FINAL JUSTICE

JOHN DEACON

Copyright © 2022 by John Deacon

All rights reserved.

No part of this book may be reproduced in any form or by any electronic or mechanical means, including information storage and retrieval systems, without written permission from the author, except for the use of brief quotations in a book review.

Final Justice is a work of fiction. Characters, names, places, and events are either the product of the author's imagination or used fictitiously. Any similarity to real persons, living or dead, is purely coincidental.

Cover design by German Creative on Fiverr

Edited by Karen Bennett

Want to know when my next book is released? SIGN UP HERE.

Created with Vellum

CHAPTER 1

"You killed my brother," a voice growled behind Justice. "Now I'm gonna kill you."

Customers in Mueller's Mercantile clucked and fluttered like so many chickens.

Justice, fearless as a fighting rooster, turned slowly.

A black-bearded man stared at him, shifting his weight back and forth, one hand on a holstered revolver.

Taking in the man's hunched posture and twitchy demeanor, Justice laid a hand casually on his own Colt. "You a Beachem?"

"That's right. Henry Beachem, brother of Harvey—who you gunned down."

Justice nodded. "I did. And now what? You want me to gun you down, too? Why not just forget it and get on with your life?"

The man shook his head. "Oh no, you're not getting out of this, mister. You want me to shoot here in the store or out in the street?"

Justice considered the innocent folks and breakable

goods around him. If Henry Beachem was fast like his brother, he'd probably get a shot off.

"Let's head outside, then," Justice said.

"Don't matter to me," Beachem said, turning toward the door. "And don't go shooting me in the back."

Justice followed him outside. He didn't want to kill this man but suspected Beachem would force it. Some men decided they had to kill or die; once they laid hold of that notion, few things could change their minds.

Out on the street, people understood instantly what was happening. Up and down the boards, people shifted their positions. Many ran for cover. Others lurked, not wanting to miss the action.

Justice went out into the middle of the street, but Beachem kept walking.

"Come on down this way a little farther," Beachem said, facing Justice but backing up. "Just a touch. Ten feet or so. Out where nobody else will get hurt."

Even before Beachem glanced up, Justice understood what was happening. There was only one reason for Beachem to lead him down the street. He was trying to draw Justice into a kill zone.

Movement flashed atop the Dos Pesos Hotel. A man rose with a rifle, brought it to his shoulder, and leaned, trying to get Justice in his sights.

A rifle boomed, splitting the moment wide.

The rooftop sniper tumbled off the hotel and slammed into the street with a crunching thump.

A panicked Beachem grabbed for his pistol. He was still clearing leather when Justice plugged him in the breastbone and put him down.

Justice moved, scanning in all directions, but detected no additional threats.

What he did see, however, was a grinning Coronado

sitting atop a good-looking chestnut down the street, his unsheathed rifle across his lap.

Justice nodded and Coronado nodded back and dismounted.

Justice had only seen the hawkish man once or twice since they first met at the raid on Tucker's place. Coronado had been right behind him, the fiercest fighter of all those who'd followed Justice into peril.

"More violence?" Sheriff Perkins said, hurrying forward with a shotgun. He had changed greatly since Justice first met him. The raid had redeemed him. Now, when gunshots exploded in Dos Pesos, he no longer cowered in his office; he ran toward them.

Justice figured there was no better measure of a man, except maybe for keeping his word and simply taking care of his family day after day, year after year.

Looking back and forth between the dead men, Perkins shook his head. "Do you leave bodies everywhere you go, Justice?"

Justice reloaded his Colt. "They're the right kind of bodies, Perkins. Bad men. Your town is safer now than it was five minutes ago. That one's a Beachem. The one over yonder was fixing to snipe me from on top of the hotel."

Perkins spat. "Henry Beachem? I believe he had some paper on him. Not much. But it'll probably cover undertaker fees."

Justice clapped him on the shoulder. "If not, let me know. I'll be in the Third Peso."

He walked over to Coronado and shook his hand.

Coronado's grip was powerful despite his size. He was short and muscular and supremely confident, like a light-weight boxing champion. He'd been a cowhand until riding against Tucker. Now, thanks to his actions that night, he owned thousands of acres and a small herd of cattle and had enough money to hire hands of his own.

"Come on over to the Third Peso," Justice said. "I owe you a beer."

"I could drink a beer," Coronado said. "But I got money now, thanks to you."

"Well, it's on me anyway. That rifleman was fixing to put a hole in me."

"Both you boys put your billfolds away. The first round's on me!" Clem crowed with characteristic exuberance. The one-armed former miner had been in Dos Pesos for a week. When he'd received word of Justice's impending nuptials, the old-timer had checked out of the Clarendon, hopped the train from Leadville, and moved into the Dos Pesos Inn.

Clem had brought with him a sizeable wedding present, Justice's $3500 reward from Marshal Dukane for killing Duke Whipple.

"No beer tastes better than free beer," Justice told his grinning friend. "I accept."

CHAPTER 2

Justice introduced Coronado to Clem, who said, "Mighty nice shooting there. I saw you aiming. Next thing I knew somebody fell out of the sky. That's the one disadvantage of watching the action from a safe haven like the inn; sometimes, you can't see everything."

The three men went into the Third Peso, where they received another surprise. None of them ended up buying the first round.

The bartender, Max Jennings, had watched the shootout through the big plate glass window. "Town's been downright peaceful since you moved in, Justice." He grinned. "Well, other than when you shoot folks, that is. Harvey Beachem was a terror, and Tucker's boys used to come in and run off all the decent customers. For us businessmen, peace is prosperity. Drinks are on me."

The men thanked Max and carried their beers to an open table in a back corner, folks nodding and saying Justice's name as they passed.

Justice put his back to the wall. Coronado grinned knowingly and sat to one side so he could keep one eye on the door. Clem jabbered away and plopped down with his back to the establishment and door alike.

They talked, catching up.

Coronado was thankful for his ranch and herd. He'd built a house, a barn, and a bunkhouse, but now he was feeling restless. "I'll always be a *vaquero* at heart," he said and took a long pull from his beer.

Justice told Coronado what he'd been up to in Leadville, Texas, and Santa Fe.

Coronado took it all in stride, having been there at Tucker's when Diego had found the telegram implicating D.G., Rose, and the late Ruble Cochran.

"So you're going to do it?" Coronado asked. "You're going to ride into Mexico after these men?"

Justice nodded. "I am. Just as soon as the wedding and honeymoon are over."

Nora had ecstatically accepted his proposal of marriage, but she refused to wait to hear from the silent justices. Whether the commander approved an exemption, or they had to live their lives on the run, she wanted to marry Justice, so why wait?

So they were getting married in three days. Justice couldn't be happier.

They'd be married in the church in Dos Pesos. Nora's mother and sisters were coming in for it.

Justice's brother, Matt, couldn't make it. He was doing well but still laid up from getting shot in the back by Cochran.

But Justice's cousin, Luke, was coming all the way from Texas to attend. It was a humbling act of kindness that surprised Justice.

Then again, what had he seen but kindness and bravery and selflessness from his family?

Nothing, that's what.

They were good people, and he looked forward to getting to know them all over again.

Neighbors Diego and Eugenia Contreras had invited Justice, Nora, Eli, and their families to dinner after the ceremony. After that, Nora's sister Faith and their mother would stay with Eli for a few weeks, giving Justice and Nora time to take a honeymoon.

The notion would have seemed ridiculous to both Justice and Nora, but they were going to New York City, where Justice needed to hunt down the Casterlin Corporation and lawyer Clarence Beales, who were protecting the identity, address, and business ventures of Don Antonio Garza, the mastermind behind the international crime ring Justice had been battling.

If he managed to track down Garza and kill Garza's top gun, Oliver Rose, Justice hoped to leverage a pardon from the commander, allowing him to walk away from the silent justices and live his life in peace with Nora and Eli and all those other kids they hoped to have.

Of course, Justice had other reasons for pursuing these men.

Don Garza had started all this trouble and called for Justice's murder.

Rose had killed Justice's pa.

So yes, this was personal. Garza and Rose needed to die.

All this aside, Justice and Nora were looking forward to having a long block of time together. He had already arranged transportation on the stagecoach to Santa Fe and trains from there. For the long ride across the country, he splurged on a Pullman berth, figuring the newlyweds would put the sleeper to good use... and not just for sleeping.

They would see the sights, eat in the finest restaurants, and stay in a fancy New York hotel. Then, after getting the information Justice needed, they would return to New

Mexico, where he would enjoy a few days with Nora and Eli before heading to Mexico, where he would serve justice and try to set their lives right.

"Where are you going in Mexico?" Coronado asked.

Justice shrugged. "Don't know yet." He explained what he planned to do in New York.

"That country down there, you have to watch yourself," Coronado said. "Before Garza, you will face Apaches, banditos, and the *rurales*."

Justice sipped his beer. "It's dangerous, but I gotta go."

"Even the land will try to kill you," Coronado said. "The heat, the cold, flash floods, lightning on the open plain. There are many ways to die in Mexico. Especially you must know where to get water. When you find out where you're going, let me know."

"I appreciate the warning."

"A warning is not enough," Coronado said. "I've been meaning to take my family some money and invite them to come live at my ranch. I will ride with you into Mexico."

"What if Garza's on the other side of the country from your people?"

Coronado grinned. "Then you will buy me even more free beer."

They shook on it. Justice would be glad for the company, especially since Coronado could fight and knew the country.

Clem polished off his beer and looked back and forth between the men, a crazy grin splitting his white beard. "If it's all the same to you boys, I believe I will sit out your adventure right here in Dos Pesos. You'll just have to survive without me. Old Clem has fallen in love."

"Love, huh?" Justice said. "I heard you'd been spending a lot of time with that red-haired saloon girl. What's her name?"

Clem bounced his snowy eyebrows up and down.

"Josephine. And yeah, I have been spending a good deal of time with her, much to Josephine's understandable delight. But when I say I've fallen in love, I'm not talking about my new lady friend. I've fallen in love with the *carne asada* at the Dos Pesos Inn. I drown it in that hot sauce that Rosa makes."

Clem lowered his hand to his stomach and winced in mock agony. "All that spice does play havoc on my innards, though."

Justice laughed. "If it tears you up so bad, why not skip the hot sauce?"

Clem leaned back and raised a brow, looking at Justice like he was crazy. "Skip the hot sauce? Now where would be the fun in that?"

CHAPTER 3

Justice rode Dagger to the barn. Rafer trotted beside them, lean and wolfish, Justice's constant multi-colored companion.

When Justice dismounted, the dog lay down in the shadows of the barn and watched him care for the stallion. Dagger was a fine horse, perhaps even the match of Bourbon back in Texas.

Eli came out to help. The boy had been grinning nonstop since Nora had told him about the upcoming wedding. This afternoon, however, the boy's smile had disappeared.

Justice pointed. "Hand me that curry comb yonder?"

Eli fetched the curry comb and handed it to him. "Justice?"

"Yeah?"

"When you marry Mama, will you be my daddy?"

Justice crouched down and looked the boy in the eyes. "No, I won't. You already have a daddy."

The boy nodded, looking disappointed. "My daddy's dead."

"But he's still your daddy."

"Yeah, I reckon so. It's just…"

"Lift your face, son, look me in the eyes. You can talk to me about anything, you hear? Now and forevermore, don't ever hesitate to unload your wagon with me."

Eli nodded. "Well, it's just, I don't know. I guess maybe I was hoping you would be my new daddy is all."

Justice put a hand on his shoulder. "Like I said, you already have a daddy. But since he isn't here to look after you now, I'm hoping you'll trust me with the job."

Eli beamed. "I'd trust you with anything, Justice."

Justice chuckled. "You have obviously never tasted my cooking, then. But you can trust my word. I make a promise, I stick to it. And I promise to take care of you and your Mama as best I can till my dying day. I will always protect and provide for you and do my best to raise you up right. I will treat you the way I would treat my natural-born son and there won't ever be an iota of difference in my mind between the two."

If Eli smiled any wider, the top half of his blond head might fall off. "I sure would like that, Justice. Does that mean I could maybe, you know, call you Daddy, then?"

"That wouldn't seem quite right to me. Your daddy is still your daddy, God rest his soul."

Eli nodded solemnly.

Justice said, "How about you call me what I always called my father?"

"What's that?"

"Pa."

Eli nodded, grinning harder than ever. "Yeah, I'd like that a lot. You'd be my pa, then."

He ruffled the boy's straw-colored hair. "I am gonna be your pa. And you're gonna be my boy. And I'm gonna teach you everything I know so you can take over this ranch someday."

———

LATER THAT NIGHT AFTER SUPPER, JUSTICE READ ELI ANOTHER chapter of *Treasure Island*. Nora joined them as she did every night and confessed that she was hooked on the story, too.

After tucking in Eli, Justice and Nora sat in the kitchen and talked over coffee, discussing the wedding and the trip to New York.

Nora's mother and sisters would arrive on the stage from Santa Fe in the morning, and Luke would be coming in from Texas later that afternoon.

Justice and Nora had bought a nice carriage that would be perfect for picking up her family. Normally, he would've just ridden out to Dos Pesos trailing a horse for Luke, but Matt had sent a telegram, explaining Justice would need a wagon because of the wedding gift Matt was sending.

When it was time for bed, they paused in the hallway and talked a little more, whispering so as not to wake Eli, and came into each other's arms and kissed softly. Their kissing grew more passionate, and they clutched each other fervently, breathing hard and wanting more.

Before they could tumble down that slope, however, Justice broke the kiss and stepped back.

Nora eyed him hungrily, her eyes wild with desire. One blond strand hung down over her pretty face, swaying as she panted for breath.

Justice wanted her like a prairie fire wants the next acre of grass, but they had already waited this long, and he knew that, despite passionate moments like these, Nora really wanted to wait for marriage before going further, so he held her at arm's reach and kissed her forehead and said, "Two more days, my love. Just two more days."

Nora bit her lip and nodded. "I feel like I'm going to explode."

"Same here. I feel like I'm packed chock full of TNT. But we can wait two more days."

"I suppose. Though I sure would like to haul you into my bed right now."

"You'd regret it."

Nora grinned. "Regret it? You're not planning to disappoint me in bed, are you?"

Justice chuckled. "I'll do my best."

She grabbed him by the shirt front. "You will be wonderful. And I can't wait. I mean, I can, and I will, and thank you for helping me to wait. It's what I want, even though I'm crazy for you. But on our wedding night, you had better look out, Mr. Bullard."

He smoothed a thumb over her pink cheek. "Is that right?"

"You know what they say about young widows."

"Actually, no, I don't know what they say."

"Well," Nora said, straightening her dress and smoothing a hand over her shapely bosom, "I'm not going to tell you what they say. I'd rather just show you when the time comes."

"I await that display with bated breath, ma'am."

She snorted. "You have no idea, sir."

CHAPTER 4

"Good to see you, Luke," Justice said, stepping forward to shake hands with his cousin.

"Good to see you, too, Jake. Never thought one of the Bullard boys would get married, but I'm happy for it. When do I get to meet your bride-to-be?"

"After we get you a beer and ride back to the ranch. Nora's family got in this morning, and they got a full-fledged hen party going on back at the house."

Luke grinned. "Maybe we'd best get two beers, then."

"I like the way you think, cousin. Let's get your luggage first."

"You might as well give me a hand," Luke said, pointing to a large wooden crate strapped to the top of the coach. "It's fixing to be yours, anyway. I'm just glad it didn't… well, don't let me go spoiling the surprise. Let's just say your brother has his ways."

Justice laughed. "That he does. How's Matt doing, anyway?"

"Good. Doc Cass has been over every day. Says every-thing's clean. No infection. Matt just has to rest up is all. Of course, telling Matt to rest is about like telling a cat to sit still in a room full of squeaking mice."

They got the crate down along with Luke's suitcase and loaded them into Justice's wagon at the livery, then walked back up the street and headed into the Third Peso, where Clem was waiting on them.

They sat for a spell, Luke slaking his thirst after the long and bumpy coach ride and telling them about everything back in Texas.

Matt was well enough to watch over the ranch, and Doc Cass would continue to check on him every day. Hostler and family friend Del Hayworth came out most days, too, just in case Matt needed anything.

Meanwhile, the Newman women were faring as well as could be hoped. They had lost their patriarch to the roving outlaws, but as predicted, the women were leaning on each other, and the money Justice and Matt had given them had been a big help. So far, they had managed to keep the whole ordeal private, just like they wanted.

When it was time to head back to the ranch, Justice asked Clem if he wanted to join them.

"I would, but I don't want to break poor Josephine's heart. She can't get enough of old Clem."

"Good luck with that," Justice said. "See you for the wedding tomorrow?"

"That's why I'm here, my friend. It's not why I'm gonna stick around, but it's why I came here."

"You're planning on hanging around Dos Pesos for a while, then?"

"Oh yeah, Josephine wouldn't know what to do without me, and somebody's gotta eat all that *carne asada*, so I reckon I'll stay here for a spell."

Justice and Luke walked back to the livery and got the

wagon and rode to the ranch, where Justice was happy to finally introduce Nora to a member of his family.

Nora embraced Luke, welcoming him warmly, saying she was overjoyed to have him as family.

Justice could see how much Nora's warmth pleased Luke. He thanked her and started to say how nice it was to meet her, but then he looked over her shoulder and saw Nora's younger sister, Faith, smiling at him and started stumbling over his words like he'd never seen a pretty girl before.

And indeed, Faith was a pretty girl. Gorgeous, even, with her pale blond hair, rosy cheeks, and bright smile and regardless of her single blemish: a dead eye that had taken a cholla spine when she was little.

Faith had always been a tomboy type, Nora had told Justice the night before. The girl was fast and tough and quick to laugh, and she rode a horse and pushed cattle like a top hand.

"She's self-conscious about her eye," Nora had told him, "but I've always thought it makes her prettier, somehow. Not the eye, exactly, but the rest of her just seems to shine all the brighter for that one flaw."

"That's the way life is," Justice had replied. "The best things aren't perfect. The best things shine despite their scars."

Based on Luke's expression, he clearly agreed.

Nora's eyes flicked between Luke and her sister, and one corner of her mouth lifted slightly. "Luke, please allow me to introduce you to my family."

Justice enjoyed watching his wife-to-be introduce her mother and siblings. He knew she was having a little fun with Luke while at the same time encouraging his interest. She saved her introduction between Luke and Faith for last, saying, "Since Faith is unmarried, she still lives with Mother… in Texas."

"Oh, Texas, huh?" Luke said, blushing. He clutched his hat at his beltline and wrung the life from it. "Texas is a nice state. I, um, live in Texas. I live there, too, I mean. What part are y'all from?"

"We live in West Texas," Faith said, smiling prettily. She did not share Luke's awkwardness, but Justice could see she did share his interest. "And what part are you from, sir?"

"Sir?" Luke laughed. "Ain't nobody ever called me sir before. Call me Luke, please."

"Well, Luke Please, call me Faith if you will."

Luke laughed and gave a little bow. "Okay, Miss If You Will."

———

THAT NIGHT AFTER SUPPER, JUSTICE, LUKE, AND ELI MOVED out to the bunkhouse, surrendering the house to the women. Together with the ranch hands, Pedro Martin and Silas Sutton, they busted out a deck of cards and taught Eli the basics of poker.

Rafer lay at Justice's feet, half-slumbering in his wolfish way.

Luke produced a bottle of genuine Jack Daniels whiskey, and every man hit it a couple of times. It was a good, relaxed night with plenty of poker, storytelling, and laughter.

Though Luke only had two shots of whiskey, he was practically drunk with his attraction to Faith. All night, he kept bringing up her name until Justice finally said, "Are you gonna ask to court her or not?"

Luke grinned. "You think I should, Jake?"

Justice spread his hands. "Cousin, the only real freedom we have in this world is making our own decisions. But if you want to court her, don't let the moment pass you by. Ask."

Luke nodded, beaming with excitement, and they both knew he'd ask the very next day.

Eli seemed even happier than Luke. He and Nora were incredibly close, but the boy loved staying up late in the bunkhouse, playing cards, and listening to these men, including his soon-to-be Pa.

Justice was the happiest of all, however. He couldn't imagine a better way to spend his last night as a bachelor and figured nothing this side of a mean bull could ruin his mood, considering he would be marrying the most wonderful woman in the world the very next morning.

CHAPTER 5

"Justice and Nora," the preacher said, "the ceremony of marriage is an ancient and holy tradition sanctified by God himself. Of your own free will you give yourselves wholly to one another for the rest of your lives, prepared to share life's burdens, comfort one another during times of sorrow, and greatly magnify the many joys of your time upon this Earth."

Justice smiled at his lovely bride-to-be, and she smiled back at him, her gorgeous blue eyes sparkling with emotion.

The preacher talked about how they were coming together, blending their hearts and lives, then told them to face each other.

Justice took Nora's hands in his. She smiled up at him, her long lashes dewy with tears of joy as the preacher got them started on their vows.

Justice stared into Nora's eyes and spoke the words. "I, Justice, take you, Nora, to be my wife, to have and to hold from this day forward, for better or for worse, for richer or for poorer, in sickness and in health, I promise to love and cherish you forever."

Nora took a deep breath, let it shudder free, and said, "I, Nora, take you, Justice, to be my husband, to have and to hold from this day forward, for better or for worse, for richer or for poorer, in sickness and in health, I promise to love and cherish you forever."

Next, the preacher recited those timeless words from *1 Corinthians 13*: "Love suffers long and is kind; love does not envy; love does not parade itself, is not puffed up; does not behave rudely, does not seek its own, is not provoked, thinks no evil; does not rejoice in iniquity, but rejoices in the truth; bears all things, believes all things, hopes all things, endures all things. Love never fails."

The preacher asked Luke if he had the ring. Luke turned to a grinning Eli, who handed him the ring. Luke passed it to Justice, who slid the plain gold band onto Nora's finger, saying, "With this ring, I seal my promise to be your faithful and loving husband, as God is my witness."

Then Nora repeated the action, sliding a gold ring onto his finger and echoing his sentiment. "With this ring, I seal my promise to be your faithful and loving wife, as God is my witness."

The preacher smiled and wrapped things up with a prayer and his own sentiments on their marriage, telling them it was a beautiful thing and wishing them and Eli all the happiness in the world.

Right about then, Justice couldn't imagine cramming one more iota of happiness into his being. He'd explode if he did, that's how happy he was.

The preacher made it official, pronouncing them man and wife, then said the words they'd both been aching to hear: "Justice, you may kiss your wife."

Their kiss was soft and sweet, almost chaste out of respect for the preacher and the friends and family gathered there today.

After the ceremony, the happy congregation mobbed them and eventually escorted them outside to where their carriage was waiting.

Luke was already in the driver's seat, grinning brightly. He stood and swept his hat from his head and gave a bow. "Mr. and Mrs. Bullard, young Master Bullard, welcome aboard the Lovey Dovey Express. My name is Luke, and I will be driving you to the residence of Diego and Eugenia Contreras for your wedding feast. Any bandits or wild Indians will be dealt with by my lovely companion and her trusty coach gun."

Beside Luke, Faith giggled, looking prettier and happier than ever.

It was a beautiful morning, sunny and mild for this time of year, as if God Himself were smiling down on their new union.

When it was time to roll out, Diego and Eugenia led the way, carting Clem along with them.

Luke followed with the happy newlyweds squeezed together on the seat and Eli smiling up at them from his mother's side.

The rest of the wedding procession followed, including the carriages Justice had rented for Nora's family, driven by Sheriff Perkins and Aaron Biscoe, who'd shown up in his old but well-maintained buffalo soldier uniform with his attractive and intelligent wife, Stephanie.

"Are you my pa now?" Eli asked.

"Yeah, I'm your pa now, son," Justice laughed, and reached across his wife to muss the boy's straw-colored hair. There wasn't as much of it to muss now, Eli's aunts having cut it this very morning in preparation for the wedding.

"Good," the boy said. Smiling, he crossed his arms over his chest and leaned back, looking very pleased indeed. "I'm glad you're my pa now."

"I'm glad, too. And proud. No man was ever prouder to call a boy his son." Then he turned to Nora. "And surely, no man was ever so proud to call a woman his wife."

They kissed, both of them anxious to get through this dinner celebration and finally be alone.

"Wanna play poker later, Pa?" Eli asked.

"Poker?" Nora said, squinting back and forth between her husband and her son. "Have you been corrupting the boy?"

"It's all right, we didn't teach him to deal off the bottom. Just a little fun between men."

"Yeah, Mama, it sure was fun."

Now, it was Nora's turn to cross her arms. She tried to look put out but failed miserably, grinning despite her attempts. "Poker," she said, and shook her head.

"To make it in the West, a man's gotta know the difference between a straight and a flush," Justice said. "Better he learns from us than from who knows who somewhere down the line."

"Yes, well—"

Justice silenced his new wife with a loving kiss, and she returned it with feeling, not minding his interruption in the least. In fact, her hand sneaked onto his thigh and gave a squeeze, fueling his desires.

But they controlled themselves as they rolled on toward the Contreras ranch, resolved to smile and chat amiably until they could escape for the night.

Before reaching the ranch, however, the procession turned unexpectedly south.

"Where we going?" Justice hollered up to Luke, who'd been chattering away nonstop with Faith.

Luke just grinned, but after traveling a short distance, Justice knew where they were headed: the headquarters of the River Valley Cattleman's Association, which had been built on the ruins of Tucker's house.

CHAPTER 6

On arrival, they were surprised to see over a hundred people—all the ranchers and their families—waiting for them. The crowd cheered as the carriage pulled to a stop. Folks lined up all the way to the steps of the headquarters to greet the newlyweds and wish them well.

Inside, in the wide-open room where the worst of the fighting had taken place, folks had set up a dining area and a big potluck dinner, buffet-style.

A table near the wall awaited Justice, Nora, Eli, and their immediate family. Everyone else spread out at the big room's many long tables.

Justice felt honored and humbled by everything that everyone had done for them. It was an incredible display of friendship and support.

Everyone plated up and waited for the preacher to say a mercifully short prayer before having at their meals.

Partway through dinner, Diego stood on a chair and got everyone's attention. People sat around grinning, looking from Justice and Nora to Diego and back again, giving Justice the feeling that they knew something he didn't know.

"Justice and Nora," Diego said, "we all wanted to get together today in honor of your wedding and to show you something. Our ranches might be spread out, but you will never be alone. Us folks here, we are your people."

All around the room, men and women nodded and the many children fidgeted as children always had and always would from the dawn of time all the way to Judgment Day.

"Anything you need, know you can come to us for help—just as we know that you will always be there to help us. In fact, you already have. Without your vision and leadership, Justice, we wouldn't be here today.

"The River Valley Cattleman's Association wouldn't even exist. Without you, this would still be Tucker's ranch. Some of us, he would've bought ought. Others, he would've forced out. Others, he would've burned out. Many of us would be dead without you. Those are the facts."

All around the room, folks looked to Justice. Men nodded and touched their hats. Women smiled, many dabbing at the corners of their eyes.

Justice waved them off. "We all did our part."

"That's enough out of you," Diego said with a grin. "This may be your big day, but this is my speech, so you kindly see your way out of it."

Laughter rippled across the room, breaking some of the tension. One of the ranchers hollered, "Yeah, Justice. Quit your yammering and let the poor man have his say."

Diego nodded at the man and continued. "Now, in light of the facts, the River Valley Cattleman's Association came together and decided to commemorate your marriage."

"You met without us?" Justice said.

Diego grinned. "I already cautioned you against speaking, Justice. I'd hate to have you ejected from your own wedding dinner."

This brought even more laughter.

But then Diego grew serious. "Coronado, you have it?"

The rugged Mexican battler nodded and stood and crossed the room and laid an envelope on the table before Justice and Nora. It was addressed to both of them in hand-writing Justice instantly recognized as belonging to their lawyer, David Spencer, who was also in attendance.

"Mr. and Mrs. Bullard," Diego said, "the River Valley Cattleman's Association hereby grants you twenty-five thousand acres adjoining your current spread along with two hundred and fifty head of cattle comprised of gifts from each and every rancher in attendance here today."

Justice was thunderstruck. This was an unbelievable gift, an inconceivable kindness. He was completely bowled over, practically stunned by the gesture.

Luckily, Nora kept her head. Justice might be the man to settle matters of life and death, but here and now in this moment demanding social decorum, she took the lead, standing and touching his arm so that he quickly joined her.

"Justice and I cannot thank you enough," Nora said, turning to show her appreciative smile to everyone in attendance. "This is quite a surprise, and please excuse me for not having the words to adequately express our grati-tude. Not that mere words could ever express the degree of gratitude we're feeling now. No, we will just have to express our thanks through our actions, from this point forward, by being the best neighbors we possibly can to each and every one of you, for so long as we all do live. Thank you, everyone. I feel like the luckiest woman in the world."

Raucous applause shook the building as if it had been struck again by dynamite.

Which was ironic because a short time later, as folks started approaching the table with wedding gifts, Luke and Faith lugged in the crate from Matt and opened it, revealing hundreds of sticks of dynamite. A note on top read, *Hope your wedding is a blast, big brother.*

Laughing, Nora said, "You Bullards certainly do appreciate weapons."

"You're a Bullard now, too, Nora," Luke said, handing her a much smaller box, "so I reckon you ought to appreciate this."

Lifting the lid, Nora smiled down at the delicate yet deadly derringer. "Thank you, Luke," she said with a genuine smile. "Now, I truly feel like a member of the Bullard clan."

———

LATER, AFTER THE BIG MEAL WRAPPED UP AND ELI WAS comfortably ensconced with his grandmother, aunts, and cousins, and Justice and Nora managed to extract themselves from all the well-wishers, the newlyweds drove off in one of the rented carriages and returned it to Manuel Chavez in Dos Pesos.

The hostler congratulated them warmly and presented Nora with a bottle of wine.

Then they went on down the street toward the room they'd rented in the Dos Pesos Inn, where their honeymoon luggage was already waiting for them. The next morning, they would have a leisurely breakfast and then catch the stage for the first leg in their long trip.

Justice was looking forward to every mile of it, every last inch of their time together.

So was Nora.

But neither of them was thinking much about the trip at this point. After navigating the lobby where the hotel staff offered their congratulations and a small cake to enjoy in their room, Justice and Nora retreated to their suite.

Justice opened the door, then scooped a laughing Nora

into his arms. He carted her over the threshold, then kicked the door shut behind them and set her on her feet again.

She smiled up at him. "Alone at last, husband."

He draped his arms over her shoulders. "Say it again."

"Alone at—"

"No, the other part."

Nora's dimples showed. "Husband."

"Yes, I'm your husband. And you're my wife. Now and forevermore."

"It's the *now* part I'm most interested in at the moment," Nora said with a sly smile, tugging him toward the bed.

CHAPTER 7

J ustice awoke to the feeling of Nora's soft lips trailing kisses across his bare chest.

"Mmm," he said. "That feels nice."

Nora smiled up at him. "Good morning, Mr. Bullard."

"Good morning, Mrs. Bullard."

He cupped her face in his hands and pulled her up and kissed her gently, loving the feel of her against him.

They had spent a wonderful night in bed, every second of it so blissful Justice could barely believe it had actually happened.

But as they continued to kiss, he not only believed it but wanted to experience it again, despite their mostly sleepless night.

"Mmm," Nora purred. "What's this? What about that leisurely breakfast you mentioned?"

"I'd just as soon get my fill of you, darlin."

Nora grinned mischievously. "Well, a wife is supposed to obey her husband, so breakfast can wait."

They ended up having just enough time to grab coffee

and biscuits before setting off on the stagecoach. Neither of them complained.

On their last trip to Santa Fe, they had met the driver, A.W. Mosely, and Carlton Traits, who rode shotgun.

For a short while, Justice and Nora had the stage to themselves. They talked about the wedding and the big party afterward, the tremendous gift of their neighbors, and the way Luke and Faith had hit it off.

"Is he a good man?" Nora asked.

"I think so. I mean, my memory's missing, but he's sure been a good man since we were reunited. He did say something back in Texas about how he'd gotten into some trouble."

"What sort of trouble?"

"I don't know. But whatever it was, he said I didn't let it bother me, that I never gave up on him. And after it was over, Matt and I still hired him to tend our ranch while we were away. Which he's been doing faithfully for some time."

"Are you worried, then, about him courting my little sister?"

"Worried? No. Most folks are a mix of good and bad. Most men, especially. And most men get into some trouble in their youth. If we held it against them forever, nobody would get married. What's important is the balance of good and bad. Some folks get a taste for the bad and keep on chasing it till it's who they are. But most folks, they have a little taste and maybe they're tempted from time to time, but in the end, they want to be good."

"That is the nature of sin."

"Yes, it is. I believe in redemption, and I believe in forgiveness. Must be I saw more good in Luke than bad because I forgave him and trusted him with my property and my animals, and he seems to have done a good job taking care of those things."

"Well," Nora said, "if you have forgiven Luke and trust him, then I have complete faith in him."

Happily exhausted, they talked and kissed and dozed lightly. Nora leaned into Justice and laid her head against his chest.

When they arrived at Embudo, Nora sat up and straightened her dress. Watching her, Justice started wishing they'd booked an extra night or two in Dos Pesos.

At the Embudo station, a severe-looking woman with a large nose, a puckered mouth, and an enormous mole on her pointy chin joined them. She wore a black dress that covered her from throat to ankle and had her gunmetal gray hair pulled back in a tight bun at the back of her unsmiling head.

Justice rose from his seat and touched his hat. "Ma'am."

The woman nodded curtly and sat across from them.

Several minutes later as Carlton Traits came hustling back from the stage station with a muffin and a cup of steaming coffee, a red-faced drummer clambered into the coach.

The sleeves of the man's threadbare jacket were frayed at the cuffs. Most of the garment, however, was covered by the large case which he clutched to his huffing chest with one arm. His tiny bowler hat was two sizes too small for his head. It titled backward, exposing his forehead, which glistened with perspiration despite the cool air and his thin jacket.

"Almost... missed it," he panted. He sat down beside the severe-looking woman, leaned back, closed his eyes, and tried to catch his breath.

The woman cast a disapproving glance in his direction, her puckered mouth tightening into what looked like a small-caliber bullet wound.

The red-faced drummer got his breathing under control but couldn't seem to get comfortable. He kept shifting around, his sales case thumping hollowly.

The woman pressed into the opposite side of the coach and scowled, apparently annoyed by every thump.

Nora bumped into Justice, smiled up at him, and whispered, "So, husband, will you finally tell me where in Santa Fe we'll be staying tonight?"

"Booked us a room at that little place we stayed at the night before you visited your sister. I remembered lying in my bed, wishing we didn't have to get two rooms."

"I remember doing the same thing. An excellent choice, Mr. Bullard."

"I'm happy you're happy, Mrs. Bullard."

They whispered together about the train schedules and connection times. Nora was excited to experience travel in Pullman berths.

Their long rail voyage would begin with the new 18-mile spur between Santa Fe and Lamy. From there, they would travel the rest of the 835-mile journey to Kansas City aboard the Atchison, Topeka & Santa Fe line. From there it would take five days to reach New York.

They would be gone for the better part of a month. They would miss Eli. The boy would miss them, too, but he was excited to spend time with his grandmother, aunts, and especially his cousins.

As they bumped along the trail a couple of miles outside of town, gunshots split the morning calm. There was a scream from above, and a shape—Carlton Traits, Justice assumed—tumbled over the side.

Justice, who'd be engrossed in conversation with his wife, quickly disentangled his arm from hers and reached for his pistol. After some deliberation, he'd decided to wear a single holster and the shoulder rig for the trip, figuring a double holster would be unnecessary and might even draw unwanted attention in the East.

But they were still in the West.

As the red-faced man proved at that moment, letting his empty case fall away and leveling a pistol at Justice's chest. "Hands off that leg iron, mister, or I'll blow you straight to Kingdom Come."

CHAPTER 8

The severe-looking woman gave a squawk of terror and leaned away from the pistol.

Justice lifted his hands. He was fast, but there was no way to beat a man who already had you dead to rights. He should've seen it coming, but he hadn't, and now he had to deal with the cards on the table.

The coach pulled to a stop. Outside, men's voices shouted.

Beside Justice, Nora squirmed but said nothing.

"That's it, mister," the red-haired man said. He was nervous and sweating like crazy, giving off waves of fear stink, but the hand holding the pistol was steady, and his eyes were hard and alert.

Justice understood this was not the man's first robbery and that he would not hesitate to pull the trigger.

"You folks just sit tight, and nobody has to get hurt," the man said. His eyes flicked to Nora, and he licked his lips. It was a curiously reptilian gesture, and suddenly, Justice wanted to kill him.

"Reach down there real easy with just your thumb and

JOHN DEACON

forefinger, mister, and pluck that shooting iron. No, not your right hand. Use your left. That's it. Real dainty like. Now don't you go doing anything stupid, or your pretty wife there is gonna be a widow." He flicked his eyes toward Nora and bounced his sweaty eyebrows up and down. "But don't you worry, sweet cheeks. We'll take care of you."

"Oh, I'm so frightened, I think I'm going to faint," Nora declared, not sounding like herself. She slumped sideways, away from Justice and started to slide toward the floor.

The man's mouth opened with surprise. The barrel of his pistol drifted slightly off target.

Justice was prepared to lash out when the coach exploded with noise and the red-faced man's head jerked backward, coming messily apart.

The severe-looking woman started shrieking and brushing frantically at her face and dress.

The man fell over. He couldn't be much deader. Justice took the pistol from his hand and drew his own Colt. His ears were ringing like crazy.

Nora got to her feet, the derringer she'd used to kill the man still in her hand.

"Here," Justice said, handing her the robber's six-shooter. "Stay onboard. Anybody comes at you, give them a frightened look and shoot them right through the door."

Nora nodded. Her eyes were huge, but she was holding it together, and he couldn't be prouder of her.

"Horace!" a man said, coming around from the front of the coach, swinging his shouldered Winchester in their direction. "Horace, everything under control back there?"

Justice shot him through the window. The rifle boomed, but the bullet went high, and the man dropped to the ground, hit hard. Justice kicked the door and charged outside, never stopping as he rushed to the front of the stage, cutting hard back and forth like a chased rabbit.

34

But he was no longer prey. Now he was the predator. The remaining bandit, who fired at him from horseback, just didn't know it yet.

The bullet whizzed by Justice's head as he returned fire, moving as he squeezed off three rapid shots.

The first missed. The second nailed the bandit in the hip. The third punched him low in the side.

The horse reared, and the bandit fell hard to the ground. He cried out in pain, spewed curses, and started to bring his pistol back around.

Before he could, Justice shot him in the chest. The man cried out and his arm jutted stiffly up, the way they sometimes do when men are killed by gunfire.

Seeing no additional threats, Justice shouted up to A.W. Mosely, "Any others?"

"No," Mosely said. "That was all of them. I think they killed Carlton. Everybody all right down below?"

"Everybody except the man who was working with them. He's robbed his last stage."

"Good," Mosely said, and spat, looking angry and disgusted. "I'm glad you killed him."

Justice didn't bother correcting him. They would have to go back to Embudo with the bodies and report everything to the law. Nora had saved them all, but if they told the truth, the papers would sensationalize everything, giving her the sort of attention she would never want.

So long as everyone thought Justice had done the killing, this would be just one more botched stagecoach robbery.

Such were the ways of the West.

CHAPTER 9

"How are you holding up, my love?" Justice asked Nora late that night when they finally settled into their hotel.

She looked at him and nodded and came into his arms and laid her head against his chest.

He held her there against him for a spell, not saying a word. It had been a long day. Traveling by stagecoach was always grueling, but that had little to do with her present state.

Nora had killed a man.

Not that the authorities knew that.

Justice had explained to Nora and the woman how they were going to play it. Neither objected, and things in Embudo went smoothly. They offloaded the dead and reported everything to the marshal, who took their statements and paid Justice a ten-dollar bounty for the red-faced man.

Then they'd gotten underway again, Justice riding up top as Traits's temporary replacement.

They had no trouble the rest of the way to Santa Fe, but they arrived a few hours later than expected.

It was almost midnight.

"I'm not sorry I killed that man," Nora said. "I wish it hadn't happened, but I'm not sorry I did it. He was ready to kill you, me, everyone. And then he would've just done it again."

Justice rubbed her back. "Some folks force your hand."

She nodded against his chest. "I'm so tired."

"That's understandable."

"I had all these high hopes for tonight. A nice dinner out then lots of fun here in the room, but now, all I feel like doing is going to sleep. Would that make you angry?"

"Angry?" he laughed. "Why in the world would I be angry? No, not at all. It's been a long day, and instead of some fancy chef-cooked meal, you ended up eating what passes for food at a stage station. Let's hit the hay, darlin. As long as we're together, I'm the happiest man in the world."

She leaned back and smiled up at him. "And I'm the happiest woman. You had better get a good night's sleep, Mr. Bullard, because you are going to need plenty of energy in the morning."

He chuckled. "Well, I'm glad my wife has a healthy appetite for such matters."

"Oh, I have a very healthy appetite. I've been starving nearly to death waiting for you all these months. I'm going to wear you out with loving."

"You keep talking that way, I'm gonna go back on my word about tonight. Then we'll see who wears who out."

Nora smiled playfully, her eyes lighting up, and he could see she was shaking off her somber mood. "Big talker."

"You think so?"

"I do."

"Oh yeah?"

JOHN DEACON

Above Nora's grin, a challenge twinkled in her blue eyes. "I think you're bluffing."

"Why don't you go ahead and take off that dress, and we'll just see who's bluffing."

———

THE TRIP TO KANSAS CITY WENT SMOOTHLY. THE FOOD WAS actually quite good, like something served by a restaurant in a big city. Justice reckoned the Atchison, Topeka & Santa Fe was going all out to compete against bigger lines.

Whatever the case, their trip across the West was wonderful and blissfully uneventful. There were no mechanical problems, no prairie fires, no trouble with bandits or Indians.

They scheduled their days around meals, which Nora loved not having to cook or clean up after, and spent the time between relaxing, talking, and making love in an unbroken celebration of their marriage and future together.

They both understood the many obstacles standing between them and the life they wanted, but whenever they talked of the future, they spoke of having overcome those challenges.

Justice knew Nora had no illusions. What she had, though, was complete confidence in him. She couldn't imagine him failing, and he had no intention of letting her down, no matter how far he had to travel or how many bad men he needed to put in the ground.

Pulling into Kansas City, they were awed by the incredible Union Depot Building. They got a suite at the Coates House Hotel on Broadway and 10th and enjoyed it so much Justice spoke to someone at the railway station and had their train reservations bumped out a day so they could stay an extra night.

Then they boarded the next train and resumed their long journey to New York. The first two days were pleasantly uneventful.

Then, at supper one night, seated toward the back of the luxurious dining car, they were surprised when a door opened behind them and a girl who looked around thirteen or fourteen years old came into the room, weeping hysterically.

Justice stood and started toward the girl, but one of the purple-vested waiters beat him to her.

"Excuse me, miss," the waiter said, sounding annoyed, "but this car is for first-class passengers only. I must ask you return to your section immediately."

"That horrible man is trying to... do things... to me," the girl sobbed.

The irritated waiter placed a hand on her back and turned her toward the door. "Get along now. You mustn't disturb our guests."

"Hold on," Justice said, laying a hand on the waiter's shoulder.

The man turned toward him with a practiced smile. "I do apologize, sir. I'm sorry if this young lady disturbed your meal. Please do return to your table. She's leaving this instant."

"Sounds to me like she needs some help," Justice said. He turned his attention to her. "Is that right? You need some help, miss?"

She nodded. "The man... tried to..."

"Sir," the waiter said, touching Justice's arm, "I am truly sorry for the disturbance. Now, miss, if you're having trouble, I must insist that you seek assistance from one of the uniformed railroad officers in your car."

Justice shook the waiter's hand from his arm and drilled him with his hardest look. "This girl needs help, and all you care about is keeping things quiet in a dining car? What kind of man are you?"

The waiter seemed to shrink. "Sir, I'm just—"

"Get back to work," Justice said. "I'll handle this. Now come on, miss. Tell me what happened and show me this man who gave you a hard time."

"Thank you, sir," she wept, clutching his arm and starting for the door.

Justice looked back over his shoulder to check on Nora. Smiling, Nora sipped her wine and gave him a little nod.

How he loved that woman.

CHAPTER 10

Between cars, Justice told the girl to stop. He wanted to know what he was getting into. "What's your name, miss?"

"Kathleen," she said, starting to get ahold of herself. "Kathleen Quinn."

"How old are you?"

"Fifteen, sir. Almost sixteen."

"Where's your family?"

She shook her head.

"They're not traveling with you?"

"No, sir. They're dead, sir. Well, my parents are dead. My brothers and sisters, we got split up. I don't know where they are. But I'm on my way to live with my uncle in New York City." Even through her tears, she smiled hopefully. "He says he'll let me stay there and feed me so long as I watch the children and work around the house."

"Well, I'm glad to hear that, Kathleen. Do you mind if I call you Kathleen?"

"Everybody calls me Katie."

"Would it be all right if I called you Katie, then?"

She nodded and smiled weakly. "Thank you for helping me, sir."

"You can call me Justice."

"Justice?"

He nodded.

"Are you a police officer?"

"Not really. But you can count on me. So I gather you are traveling alone to see this uncle of yours, Katie?"

She nodded. "I was excited for the trip, but then I ended up sitting next to this horrible man, and he's been saying things to me. Awful things. And in the night, he was… well, I woke up, and he was touching me."

An inferno of rage burned within Justice, but he just nodded and offered what he hoped was a comforting smile. "I'm sorry to hear that, Katie. No man has the right to do anything like that to you."

"That's what I told him. He would stop for a while, but then he would start up again. Just a moment ago, he said the worst things to me so I got up and walked out of the car, just to get away from him. And he followed me and caught me in the next car, and it was empty, and he pushed me down on a seat and started to undo his britches, but I slipped out and came into the dining car. I'm awful sorry for upsetting your meal, but—"

"Don't even mention it. You did the right thing, and I am so very glad to meet you and be in a position to help. Now, please take me to this man so I can make sure he doesn't bother you anymore."

Suddenly, Katie looked afraid. "He's a big man, Justice. Not as tall as you but big and strong. I don't want you to get hurt."

Justice smiled. "Thank you for your concern, Katie, but I think I'll be okay. I've dealt with men like this before. Many times, in fact."

"All right. Thank you, Justice. You're like a knight in shining armor."

"A knight in shining armor?" he laughed.

"Don't mind me. I guess I'm just silly. But at the orphanage, they had a little library of books, and I loved to read about those old times. King Arthur and the Knights of the Round Table, Ivanhoe, all those old stories. I used to lay in bed at night and wish a knight would come and save me." She laughed self-consciously. "But now I'm prattling on like the village idiot. You must think I'm feeble minded."

"I don't think that at all, Katie." He was happy to see her recovering from her ordeal, but he wanted to deal with this brute so bad his knuckles ached. "Now, this man, is he in the next car?"

She nodded, looking frightened again. "He might be gone, but yes, that's where he was, where he tried to…"

"It's okay, Katie. Let's go ahead. I'd like you to identify him. Then you can step back out here and wait, and I will take care of everything. That's a promise."

"Thank you, Justice."

He opened the door to the empty car, and Katie stepped inside. Justice hung back, watching and listening, concealed by the doorway.

"There you are, you little harlot," a burly man around Justice's age said, coming out of one of the nearby seats. "Decided you wanted it after all, huh? Doesn't matter one way or the other to me. I'm getting what I want, you little—who in the blazes are you?"

Justice stepped past Katie, patting her gently on the shoulder. "Go ahead and wait where we were talking, Katie. This will only take a moment."

Without a word, the girl fled the car and closed the door behind her.

"What's the big idea?" the man said, stalking forward,

glowering at Justice, his big fists swinging at his sides. "Get your own tart. She's mine."

Smiling, Justice shook his head. "She's not a tart. She's a child. And you are filth of the lowest order."

"You just made a big mistake, buddy," the man sneered. He reached for Justice's shirt front with one hand and drew the other back in a massive fist.

"No," Justice said, latching onto the wrist of the reaching hand. "You're the one who made a mistake."

He yanked hard on the man's arm, pulling him sharply toward him. In the same instant, he threw a lightning-quick left jab that raced inside the startled man's awkward haymaker.

Justice's knuckles shot under the man's protruding chin and slammed into his throat.

The man dropped, gurgling and clutching his throat.

Justice brought his bootheel down hard on the man's groin.

The man gave a strangled shriek.

Justice brought his bootheel down again and again, stomping the man's hand, his ribs, his face. A scoundrel like this wasn't worth breaking his knuckles on.

When the man passed out, Justice bent and rolled him over, then grabbed him by his belt and collar and hauled him up and started dragging him down the aisle toward the door opposite of where Katie waited. She didn't need to see this.

The man was big, over two hundred pounds, but Justice was so angry the man felt light as a bale of winter-dry straw.

When they reached the other end of the car, the man came to, jerking around and shaking his head.

Justice slammed him into the wall and opened the door, exposing the gap between cars. The man struggled, but Justice bulled him through the opening into the rush of frigid, smoky air outside.

"Enough," the man said, "I didn't mean anything. She's yours."

"Man like you, you don't even deserve to live," Justice said. "You're lucky I don't have my Bowie, or I'd geld you here and now."

"Please," the man blubbered, "leave me alone."

"That's what she told you," Justice said, "but did you listen? No. Remember how this feels and don't ever abuse another girl for the rest of your miserable life."

Justice gave the weeping, musclebound scoundrel a hard shove. With a scream, the man flew from between the cars, disappearing into the night.

Justice leaned out and by the light of the passenger cars behind him watched the man tumble away, bouncing hard on the desolate prairie.

The last Justice saw of him, the man was up on his feet, reaching out to the train, which sped on through the night.

Then Justice went back into the empty car, strode its length, and straightened his clothes before opening the door at the other end and smiling down at a hopeful-looking Katie.

"Is everything all right, Justice?"

"Yes, it is. He won't ever bother you again."

"Oh, thank you so much."

"It was my pleasure. Truly. Now, have you eaten?"

"I had a sandwich yesterday."

"A sandwich. Yesterday."

"Yes sir," she said.

Only now that the crisis was over did he realize just how malnourished the poor girl looked.

"Katie, would you do me a favor and join my wife and me for dinner tonight?"

CHAPTER 11

"I am so very pleased to make your acquaintance, Katie," Nora said when the girl joined them.

Katie smiled and thanked her and gave a little curtsy then joined them at the table. The waiter looked like he had swallowed his bow tie. But he came over nonetheless, cast a wary glance at Justice, and said, "Will the young lady be joining you this evening, sir?"

"That's right."

"I will return at once, miss, with a place setting and soup. Would you care for fresh bread?"

Katie's eyes lit up. "Yes, please."

"For dinner," the waiter said, "would you prefer pot roast or a pork chop?"

Katie's eyes glowed all the brighter. She turned them to Justice with a hopeful look.

"You go ahead and get whatever you like, Katie. Get them both if you want."

Katie giggled and ordered the pot roast.

Nora engaged her in conversation and soon, they were chattering happily away.

Justice was impressed by how quickly the girl had overcome her earlier distress. But when you're hungry—truly hungry—and also starved for kindness, simple comforts could work miracles.

The waiter returned, set Katie's place, and brought her soup and a basket of fresh bread. The girl thanked him and stared at the food with bulging eyes.

"Have at it," Justice said.

Katie bowed her head in silent prayer, selected a piece of bread, and sampled her soup with a smile.

Despite her obvious hunger and humble past, she sat up straight and displayed impeccable manners.

"You dissuaded the man?" Nora asked Justice quietly.

"He decided to disembark early."

Nora muffled her laughter with her cloth napkin then returned to questioning the girl.

Katie proved to be a pleasant dinner companion. She had been living at the orphanage for nearly two years. She loved to cook and read, she explained, and was incredibly grateful to her uncle for summoning her. She didn't know the man, but the thought of having a home among family thrilled her.

"It sounds like he needs help, too," she explained. "He is a widower with five young children."

"Your cousins," Nora said with a smile.

"Yes, ma'am, I suppose they are. I will be caring for them and helping with housework and cooking. In return, my uncle will feed me and give me a place to stay."

"Well, I'm very happy for you," Nora said.

Later, after Justice had escorted Katie back to her seat, Nora said, "That was very kind of you, husband. Did you really throw him off the train?"

"He's lucky I didn't snap his neck first. I got no use for a man who'll force himself on a woman, let alone a child."

Nora nodded. "Next time, go ahead and snap his neck first."

―――――

THE REST OF THE TRAIN TRIP WAS PURE JOY.

They lounged and talked and made love and enjoyed talking to folks from all over.

They invited Katie to join them for every meal. She was hesitant at first, not wanting to impose, but Nora insisted, and the girl was overjoyed.

She was a sweet, well-mannered child, who smiled through her sorrow. Justice respected her bravery and optimism and found her comical because the more she talked, the more she revealed her whimsical side. A true lover of books, she hoped her life in New York would be a grand adventure.

Justice reckoned she would have her work cut out for her with all those kids and all that housework, but he kept those thoughts to himself, figuring this was a girl who had survived on dreams of a brighter future, bless her soul.

When they reached New York City, they offered to escort Katie across town to her uncle's apartment. Justice was glad they were there to help the girl and wondered what kind of a man her uncle was to let her fend for herself in this chaotic place.

They hailed a carriage. A short time later, Justice realized it wouldn't have taken much longer to walk. Thanks to the congested streets, the carriage moved very slowly and stopped frequently.

He did not regret the rental, however, because it saved the ladies from having to walk and meant he didn't have to carry the luggage. Besides, going by carriage allowed him to study this strange place.

New York teemed with humanity and reeked of heaped manure. People came and went in droves along manure-strewn streets hedged by towering buildings. There were folks of all types here, the rich and poor of countless ethnicities.

Crossing town, he caught snippets of German, French, Spanish, and Chinese, along with several languages he didn't recognize.

There were children everywhere. Most of them were dirty and ragged and boisterous, running in packs like feral creatures.

Orphans, he thought. *This city's full of orphans.* It made him all the happier that Nora and he could escort Katie to her uncle's.

Onboard the train, sitting up and chatting, Katie had seemed like a little lady. Here, among the filth and orphans and discordant crowds, she seemed smaller and younger and more vulnerable. Gone were the bright smile and optimistic dreams. This place had reduced her again to a frightened child.

It was odd how quickly things changed from block to block. In the nicer neighborhoods, things were quieter, and folks were clean and dressed up real fancy. The crowds thinned and the orphans disappeared, replaced by visible police officers and sanitation crews shoveling manure and sweeping the walks. Overhead, the air was busy with telegraph cables and what Justice guessed were electrical wires. He'd heard that some sections of the city now had electric lights.

That notion had interested him back in the West. Now, after only a short time in this sprawling city, he reckoned they could have their electric lights. He'd stick with coal lamps and campfires, along with the peace and quiet of life on the ranch.

The whole of this crazy place, all these people packed together like rats with the stink and filth and ubiquitous orphans, felt like an omen of things to come if this young nation wasn't careful. Justice was no powerful thinker, but if this city, which folks back West regarded as the pinnacle of civilization, represented the nation's future, the people of this great land had all made a wrong turn at some point.

He was still hoping to show Nora a good time here. That being said, he had already had his fill of New York City and couldn't wait to get back to the open range.

By the way Katie had talked, Justice expected to find her uncle's home in one of the quiet, fancy neighborhoods, but the carriage dropped them on a filthy street of buckling cobblestone that smelled of manure and urine. It was a neighborhood of rowhouse tenements populated by Irish immigrants and patrolled by packs of rough-looking boys. Though it was only midday, drunks lounged on stoops and slept on the sidewalks. Women peered from broken windows like mice peeking from holes in uninsulated walls.

Justice knew poverty. In the West, poverty was expected, a thing as common as living and dying. Folks bore up under it and scratched a living out of the earth.

This brand of poverty, however, was altogether different. It cast deep shadows that teemed with corruption and sin and danger.

He was seized with a wild desire to just keep on walking and save Katie from this place. By the look on Nora's horrified face, she was thinking the same thing.

But they did their duty and marched up the steps to the uncle's residence. Katie was frightened, Justice could see, but she put on a brave face and battled back the tears, realizing it was time to part ways with her new friends.

"Don't forget to write," Nora said. "Justice and I will return to New Mexico in a few weeks. And we do hope that you will find time to visit one day, as we said. We will pay for your trip, of course."

"Thank you both so much for everything," Katie said, embracing Nora and shaking Justice's hand. "I don't know what would have become of me if you hadn't shown up when you did. It was an answer to prayer."

"Well, we are much the richer for having made your acquaintance," Nora said, and Justice nodded in agreement.

"You take good care of yourself, Katie," he told her, "and let us know if you ever need anything."

Katie thanked them again and knocked on the door.

A moment later, the door swung open, and a fierce looking, bedraggled woman with a black eye and a crying baby in each arm snapped, "What do you want?"

"Excuse me, ma'am, but I'm—"

The woman cut her off with a peel of nasty laughter. "Oh, you're the niece, ain't you? The orphan girl? Mother, Mary, and Joseph, you've made it. It's about time." She hauled Katie inside and slammed the door.

"I hate leaving her like this," Nora said.

Justice nodded. "Me, too."

"But I suppose we've done all we can. At least she has a home with family."

"Yeah, I reckon you're right, but it doesn't sit well, does it?"

"Not at all. I miss the ranch, Justice."

"So do I, my love. So do I. Maybe we'll finish up our business here quickly and head home early."

Nora beamed at that notion. "That sounds wonderful."

"We'll see what we can do. The Casterlin Corporation's headquarters are only a short walk from our hotel." They started up the street, but he paused to glance back toward the uncle's apartment. "Whenever we leave, though, I reckon maybe we ought to stop back by here and make sure Katie's okay. I want her uncle to understand she's not alone in the world."

"I agree," Nora said. "Should we say something to him now?"

"No. Let him show his true colors first. We'll check on her in a couple of days."

CHAPTER 12

"Well, this hotel is certainly nice, anyway," Nora said, leaning forward so Justice could scrub her back. The tub was big enough to fit both of them at once. To fill it, they simply opened the tap and out came hot water.

"It sure is," he said, lifting the blond locks at the back of her neck and washing her shoulders. "Now, if you could plop this setup down about a mile outside of Dos Pesos…"

She laughed.

Bathing and spending some private time alone in the room helped them feel grounded again.

Later that afternoon, they took a short walk to Fifth Avenue, where they stared up at a small brass plate above the arched doorway of a stately stone building.

Casterlin Corporation.

"Well, this is it," Justice said and tried the door.

It was locked.

He knocked.

There was no answer.

He knocked again.

Still no answer.

Nora gave the door a dubious look. "Strange that a corporation wouldn't be open on a weekday afternoon."

"Yeah, that's not the only strange thing about this outfit. We'll try again later. What do you say we get an early supper?"

They decided to try Delmonico's. Justice offered to hail a carriage, but Nora wanted to walk. "We've sat so much since leaving home, it feels nice to stretch my legs."

He agreed. Taking her arm, he headed for the restaurant. This section of New York was mostly businesses. They kept things nicer here, and things felt calmer, though some of that feeling might have been due to their time relaxing in the hotel.

Manhattan was easy to navigate, thanks to its sensible grid of streets and avenues, and they soon arrived at the restaurant, where they ordered steaks, mashed potatoes, and wilted spinach salad with walnuts and cranberries and a light vinaigrette dressing.

Nora had two glasses of wine, and Justice had three beers. They took their time, chatting and sipping and savoring their food, which was quite good. The service was excellent, too.

Nora glanced around the room at all the wealthy people in their fancy clothes eating their expensive meals. "This is nice, Justice. Thank you for bringing me here."

He reached across the table and laid his hand atop hers. "I'll take you wherever you want to go, darlin."

"As long as I'm with you, I don't care where we are," Nora said, "but I will cherish this memory forever. Do you miss Eli?"

"You know I do. You?"

She sipped her wine and nodded. "I miss him horribly. We've never been apart before. Not for this long. It's taxing."

"I'm sure. You two are pretty tight."

"We sure are. He's my constant companion. I'm sorry, Justice. I don't mean to cast a shadow over this dinner."

"You're not. It's good to talk about the boy. I'll bet he misses you."

Nora shrugged. "Probably. If I know Eli, though, it comes and goes. Most of the time, I suspect he's having too much fun with his cousins to worry about his mother. Do you think we'll have a boy or a girl?"

"Both, I hope. Lots of each."

"No, I mean now."

"Now? You think you're pregnant?"

She smiled. "I know I'm pregnant."

"How in the world could you know you're pregnant? We've only been married a little over a week."

She spread her hands. "A woman knows. I'm pregnant. You just wait and see, Mr. Bullard."

Justice smiled at her. "I hope you are right, Mrs. Bullard. And I hope it's a girl, a girl who looks just like her beautiful mama."

"You keep sweet talking me like that, Mr. Bullard, and I'm going to drag you back to the hotel and have my way with you."

Justice laughed loudly enough to draw the eyes of those seated at nearby tables. "Drag away. I'm ready and willing."

After dinner, Nora ordered a custard with fresh raspberries on top, and Justice got a cup of coffee.

By the time they paid and left the restaurant, it was late and most of the businesses were shut for the night. Electric lights illuminated the main thoroughfares, but the alleyways were dark.

A cold wind blew in from the west. Nora shivered, and Justice pulled her close.

"That air is damp," Nora remarked. "It chills my bones."

"We'll cut through these alleyways, then. The wind's coming west to east, and they run north to south. Besides, they're tighter. The walls will block the breeze."

"You won't get lost?"

"Nah. Our hotel's that way. We'll head south through the alleys until we hit our street. Then we'll take a right."

"All right. I trust you, husand."

They stuck to the alleys, moving parallel to the wider avenues but staying out of the wind, which they felt all the more each time an alley ended and they had to cross one of the main streets.

Halfway down an alley just two blocks from their street, a dark shape moved from the shadows and blocked their path.

"You gotta pay a toll to use this alley," a gravelly voice said. Steel glinted in the shadows.

Behind them, a door opened, and two more figures stepped into the alley, blocking any chance of retreat.

"Yeah," one of the newcomers said. "Pay up."

If things had been different—if Justice had been alone; if it had been light enough to see what these men were carrying; if there had only been one of them instead of three—Justice might have tried talking his way out of this situation.

But he wouldn't risk Nora's life for the sake of shadow-dwelling scum like this.

Without a word, he drew his Colt and fired, knocking the first man over, then grabbed Nora, pulled her behind him, and fired again, dropping another of the men. The third man cried out, scrambled back inside, and slammed the door, abandoning his friends.

There truly is no honor among thieves.

"Come on," Justice said, taking Nora's arm and stepping wide around the first man, who lay gurgling in the darkness. Further back, the other man he'd shot moaned wordlessly.

"The one who got away might be fetching a scattergun or some friends. Either way, let's get out of here."

"What about the other two?"

"They brought this upon themselves. Now, they can deal with the consequences."

CHAPTER 13

The next morning, Justice and Nora slept in then caught breakfast at a diner just down the street. Justice was still full from the big steak dinner the night before, so he stuck with bacon, toast, and coffee, but Nora woke with an appetite and ordered eggs, sausage, and home fries with buttered toast and sliced melon on the side. Like her husband, she also drank a good deal of piping hot coffee.

Such was the nature of their lives that they barely even spoke of the previous night's alleyway incident. Both of them were conditioned to violence now the way a northerner is conditioned to cold. It was an unpleasantness that came and went. You did what you could and kept moving, and there wasn't much sense talking about it unless there was something to be learned.

They had learned nothing from the night before, of course, and Justice felt no remorse, no pity, and no curiosity as to the fate of the men he'd shot in self-defense. They had gotten what they deserved.

After breakfast, they headed back to Fifth Avenue, where the door of the Casterlin Corporation remained locked.

Justice knocked. Again, there was no response.

"We'll try them again later," Nora said.

Justice studied the door doubtfully. "They won't be here. Or at least they won't answer their door. These folks specialize in not answering doors."

"How do you mean?"

"Well, I'm starting to think that's the whole purpose of this outfit. They don't just hide the identities and dealings of folks like Garza. That's their sole purpose. They're like a hidey-hole for rich folks working on the wrong side of the law."

"If that's the case, how can they afford an office on Fifth Avenue in Manhattan?"

"Oh, if there's one thing folks like this have in spades, it's money. We're wasting our time here. Let's track down that Casterlin lawyer Doc told me about, Clarence Beales, and see what he can tell us."

They headed east again. Once more, Justice suggested hailing a carriage, and once more, Nora said she preferred to walk.

When they reached Fifth Avenue, they tarried, strolling a few blocks, peering into the great glass storefronts of the impressive stone buildings.

"Where do these folks get all their money?" Nora asked, pausing before a twinkling jewelry store display. "You suppose they were born into it?"

"I have no idea, but I know where we get our money."

She smirked at him. "Selling cattle."

"That and killing bad men."

"I look forward to a day when we can just sell cattle."

"So do I," he said, meaning it, though no sooner had the words left his mouth than he had to wonder if they were true. Yes, he had spoken the truth, but would he really be happy as a full-time rancher?

Perhaps. He certainly would love spending all his time around Nora and their children.

But Justice was more than his name, more than his profession; justice was his soul. Could he really leave its dispensation to others?

He didn't know, couldn't know until things shook out. They'd see how it all went. First, he had to get Garza, which meant finding this Clarence Beales.

"Look at that pendant," Nora remarked, shaking her head. "Have you ever seen such a large sapphire?"

"You want it?"

"Want it?"

"Yeah, that's what I'm asking. If you want that necklace, let's go in there, and I'll buy it for you right now."

Nora laughed. "Oh, Justice, you do spoil me. No, my love, I do not want that necklace. I am a rancher."

"What's that have to do with anything?"

"A rancher doesn't need such a thing. What would I do, wear it to impress the mules?"

"You could wear it whenever you wanted. You could wear it into Dos Pesos or when we meet with the cattleman's association."

"You're sweet, Justice, but I have no interest in such possessions. I wouldn't even enjoy a thing like that. Every time I saw it, I would think of all the sensible things we could've done with the money."

Justice shrugged. "I happen to agree. I've never seen much sense in things such as that, but if you want something, I'll buy it for you."

"Well, in that case, Mr. Bullard, I could probably use some more flour and sugar when we get back to Dos Pesos. I just know Mother is baking pies and cookies for those children every day."

They crossed Fifth and continued east for a few blocks, coming to a strip of elegant stone homes between 2nd and 1st.

"Nice neighborhood," Nora remarked.

"Yup, not an orphan or a horse apple in sight. This one's his."

He walked up the stone steps and rapped the iron knocker.

A short time later, the door opened, and a dour-looking man in a tuxedo stared down his nose at them. "Yes? How may I help you?"

"We're here to see Mr. Beales," Justice said.

The man blinked, then looked back and forth between them. Some folks, they don't have to say anything, don't even have to change their expression, and you can feel the contempt coming off them. This guy was one of them. "Who may I say is calling?"

Justice gave him half a grin. "Will that change whether he's here or not?"

"Mr. Beales is not available at this time, sir. If you would care to leave your name, he will contact you at his earliest convenience."

"No, I'm gonna talk to him now."

The butler's frown grew severe. "Sir, you don't seem to understand—"

"I understand perfectly. You're the one with the hearing problem. I'm going to talk to Beales right now."

The butler lifted his chin and flared his nostrils. His eyes flashed with offense. "Good day, sir."

He started to close the door in their faces, but Justice stuck out his boot and jammed it open.

"Sir," the butler said, struggling to push against the door. "I must insist—"

Justice squeezed into the gap, got his back against the

jam, and shoved the door full open, driving the butler backward.

A middle-aged man in spectacles and a plaid waistcoat stepped into the hall with a confused expression. "What is the meaning of this?"

"You Beales?" Justice said, marching toward him.

The man lifted his chin. "I am Clarence Beales. Why are you invading my home? Winston, fetch the chauffeur."

"Winston," Justice said, drawing back his coat so the butler could see his Colt, "you stay put, you hear me?"

"Yes, sir."

Justice looked past Beales into the room he'd stepped out of and saw a lot of polished mahogany and floor-to-ceiling shelves stuffed with leatherbound books. "Now, both of you, get in the library."

The men complied.

Justice followed, saying, "Darlin, do you still have that pocket pistol?"

"I sure do."

"You remember to reload after you shot that man on the way here?"

"Of course, my dear."

Justice flashed her a quick smile then locked the door behind them. "Keep your pistol on the butler."

The Remington was in her hand now. She pointed it at the man then gestured toward the corner. "Over there, Winston. My husband has business with your employer."

"Sir," Beales said. "There is no need for violence. I have money if—"

"I don't want your money."

"You don't?" Beales said, clearly confused.

"Folks like you, all you think about is money. You'll do anything for it. Even protect criminals. Smugglers, murderers, men who are exploiting young women."

"I don't have any idea what you're talking about," Beales lied.

"Yeah, you do. You know exactly what I'm talking about. The Casterlin Corporation."

Beales doubled down on his confused act, adding an offended look and a touch of haughtiness. "The Casterlin Corporation is a well-respected organization that—"

"Helps men like Antonio Garza to sell young girls into prostitution."

Beales's mouth dropped open. "I assure you, sir, we never—"

"Spare me your lies, Beales. Men like you specialize in lying. But now I'm here. You know what I am?"

Beales shook his head.

"I am the truth. And I am Justice."

"I've done nothing wrong, sir."

"You've done plenty wrong, but lucky for you, I'm not here to make you pay. I just need some information from you is all."

"Information?"

"Tell me where to find Antonio Garza."

"I'm sorry, sir. The Casterlin Corporation does not surrender information concerning its clients."

"You're about to make an exception."

Summoning his courage, Beales scowled at Justice. "I will do no such thing. You think you can come in here and bully me into surrendering information about a client? Preposterous! You have no authority, sir!"

"You're wrong, buddy. I got plenty of authority. Here, let me show you." With lightning quickness, Justice slapped the man hard across the face, knocking his glasses to the floor and sending him stumbling into a bookshelf.

Justice took a little off the slap, not wanting to knock the guy cold. It wasn't easy, pulling it, not when he was so angry at this heartless protector of the vile.

Winston gasped.

Nora laughed.

Beales pressed a hand to his red cheek and started weeping.

"You fancy New York lawyers sit over here in the East, thinking you can do whatever you want with the West and all us poor folks over there. Well, Mr. Beales, today the West has come a'callin. And the West needs you to understand that from this day forward, we will hold you and your corporation personally responsible for the actions of men like Garza. Now, where can I find him?"

"I would tell you if I knew," Beales wept. Justice could see the lawyer was lying again. "But I don't have his address."

"In that case," Justice said, reaching into his pocket, "say goodbye to the West and say hello to the Wild West."

With a theatrical flick of the wrist, Justice snapped open his clasp knife. "You don't tell me Garza's address, I'm gonna scalp you."

Beales shrieked, his mouth twisting with horror as he clapped both hands atop his head.

Smiling like a maniac, Justice stepped forward, holding up the blade so it winked in the light. "I've never scalped a lawyer before."

"What about that fella in Topeka?" Nora asked, playing along perfectly. "Wasn't he a lawyer?"

"Nah, that was a judge. Now what's it gonna be, Beales? The address or your scalp?"

CHAPTER 14

Later, Justice and Nora went to a plain old diner for supper. They were both sick of New York's elite and just wanted to fill their bellies and talk.

"For as tired as I am of posh restaurants," Nora said, stealing a sip of Justice's beer, "when you change our reservations, can we still get a Pullman berth? I don't feel like sleeping sitting up all the way back to New Mexico."

"Of course," Justice said. "Only the best for my wife. You put on a real show today. You'd make quite the silent justice."

Nora laughed and shook her head. "You know, I've always abhorred violence, but with you, it's different. You only hurt folks who have it coming."

"That's the idea. Guys like Beales, they make it possible for Garza to kidnap young girls and sell them to brothels across the border. You tell me, how lucky is he to get away with a slap in the face?"

"Very lucky indeed. You don't think he'll tell Garza?"

Justice shrugged. "I reckon I made it pretty clear what would happen if he did. I think he believed me, too."

Nora laughed. "Oh, he believed you. When you told him what you'd do, he turned whiter than a winter weasel."

Ultimately, Beales had provided two addresses, one in Piedras Negras, the other south of New Mexico in Chihuahua. The terrified lawyer had also told them that Garza spent the bulk of his time in the Chihuahuan *hacienda*. The Piedras Negras address was more of a business location, a place to meet with American clients visiting from across the border.

Now, Justice couldn't wait to get back home, tell Coronado, saddle up, and hit the trail.

This desire did not, however, impact his evening, which he and Nora enjoyed immensely.

He offered to take her to a play, but Nora just wanted to stay in their room instead.

That suited Justice just fine.

———

"Here we are, sir," the coachman said, pulling to a stop in front of the decrepit home of Katie Quinn's uncle. "Shall I wait for you?"

"Yes, please wait," Nora said. "We'll only be a minute."

"Very well, ma'am."

Justice gave his wife a hand down and held her arm as they climbed the stairs and knocked on the door.

After a short while, the door jerked open, and there stood the unpleasant dark-haired woman, still holding a crying baby in each arm. "We don't want any," she said, and started to close the door.

As he had at the lawyer's house, Justice jammed the door open with his boot. "Hold on there, ma'am. We're here to check on—"

"Justice! Nora!" Katie cried rushing toward them.

Nora gasped at the sight of the girl, and Justice gritted his teeth.

Katie still wore the same dress, only now it was spattered and stained. Her copper-colored hair hung limply around her face. The thing that really drew his attention, however, was the massive shiner she was sporting. Her left eye was swollen completely shut, the lids as rounded, taut, and purple as the curves of a summer plum.

"What happened, Katie?" Nora asked as the poor girl came into her arms.

"She fell down the stairs," the woman sneered.

"She wasn't asking you," Justice said. "What happened, Katie?"

"My uncle isn't nice," Katie sobbed. "He drinks and—"

"He hit you?"

Katie nodded. "It hurt really bad, Justice. Worse than anything ever. I can't see out of that eye, and I've had a headache ever since."

"Welcome to the world, honey," the vicious woman chuckled bitterly. "Your uncle's a man. Of course he drinks. Of course he hits us. We're just women, ain't we?"

"Where is he?" Justice said, pushing past the woman.

"He ain't here. He's working."

"Where?"

"Down the block at the butcher's." Her dark eyes twinkled with interest. "You gonna let Seamus have it, mister?"

"That's his name? Seamus?"

The woman nodded. "Don't tell him I sent you. I need this job. You go down there, Seamus will be there. He's kind of bald on top with a big, black mustache."

"Come on," Justice said.

"No, please," Katie begged. "Don't leave me."

"We aren't leaving you, sweetie," Nora said. "We're taking you with us."

"Taking me where? I have no place to go."

"Yes, you do. You can come live with us. You can help us around the ranch and help me prepare meals."

Katie blinked at her, not comprehending. "You would do that for me?"

"Of course," Nora said. "You're a wonderful child, and you deserve a good life."

"And you don't mind, Justice?" Katie asked.

"I'd love to have you with us," he said. "We'll fill your room with books."

That was the final straw. Katie burst into happy tears, and Nora led her back into the filthy apartment to gather her few meager possessions.

"Hey, mister," the black-haired woman said. "You got room for me, too? I'm great with kids." She gave the howling babies a bounce to demonstrate.

"No thanks," he said, "we're full up."

When Katie and Nora came back out, he took the girl's tiny bag and escorted them out of the house and back to the carriage. Giving them a hand up, he set the bag beside Katie and glanced down the street, where he spotted the butcher shop.

"I'll be right back," he said, and strode away, eating the distance with every swing of his long legs.

Justice threw open the door to the butcher shop, startling the young man behind the counter. "Where's Seamus?"

"In the back. Can I help you, sir?"

Justice started around the counter, meaning to go into the back, when Seamus emerged. Justice knew it was him by his balding head and drooping mustache. A thickset, sullen-looking man in a bloody apron, he glared at Justice while wiping his big hands on a bloodstained towel. "Who are you?"

"You Seamus?"

The man nodded. "What is it to—"

Justice lashed out and nailed him in the forehead with the heel of his palm.

Seamus staggered back, cursing.

Justice was on him, driving hard hooks into his body. He spoke as he delivered these crushing blows. "Teach... you... not... to... beat... women... and... children."

With each snarled word, Justice slammed another punch into the grunting butcher's gut and sides, snapping ribs beneath the girdle of fat.

Justice caught movement out of the corner of his eye and saw the kid stepping tentatively in his direction, a meat cleaver raised overhead, trembling in midair.

An instant later, Justice's Colt was in his hand, leveled on the kid's chest.

The kid's eyes went wide, and he dropped the cleaver to the floor.

"You just back on up, son," Justice said. "I don't want to hurt you. I'm here for this pig. He beats women and children. Swelled his niece's eye clean shut."

Clutching his side and cursing, Seamus tried to rise.

Justice kicked him in the face, targeting the same eye Seamus had blackened on Katie. The brow split and the eye ballooned instantly with swelling.

Justice pressed the muzzle of his Colt into Seamus's forehead. "I'm taking your niece away and giving her a better life. You hear me?"

"Take the stupid—"

Justice whacked him across the bridge of the nose with the barrel of his Colt.

Seamus cried out.

"You just mind how you speak of Katie," Justice said. "Someday, I'll be back. First thing I'm gonna do is check your house, see how you're treating the women and children. I hear you're hurting them again, I'm gonna take you in the back of this shop and grind your hands into hamburger. You hear me?"

Fifteen seconds later, Justice closed the door, climbed aboard the carriage, and told the driver to get rolling.

He had to get out of this corrupt city. Otherwise, he'd have to spend every waking moment doling out Western justice. The unjust dead would block the streets like a logjam.

New York City was beyond salvation.

CHAPTER 15

E li practically tackled his mother when they returned to the ranch. Nora picked him up and spun him around and said she barely recognized him because he'd gotten so big.

The long trip home from New York went smoothly, giving Justice and Nora time to get to know Katie, and giving the girl time to heal and recover from her harrowing experience in New York.

Justice rented Katie her own Pullman. Embarrassed by her eye and the state of her clothing, the girl hid away in her berth most of the time, reading books borrowed from the train's impressive library.

She read quickly, devouring *Little Women*, *Jane Eyre*, *Wuthering Heights*, and *The Three Musketeers*, and enthusiastically telling Justice and Nora all about them over the meals they shared.

They spent a couple of days in Kansas City. Nora took Katie shopping and bought her more books, new clothing, and everything else a young woman would need.

Before leaving Kansas City, they asked Katie if she was

certain she wanted to continue with them to New Mexico. Justice offered to take her back to the orphanage and speak to the nuns.

"Please don't make me go back," Katie begged. "I want to stay with you both in New Mexico. I promise I'll be good. I'll do all my chores and never cause any trouble and—"

Nora interrupted her by hauling the poor girl into a hug. "You are more than welcome to come live with us like a daughter, Katie. We aren't trying to get rid of you. We just want you to know it's your choice. That's all."

"If it's my choice, I will go with you and never, ever leave."

Now she was here with them, standing beside Justice, smiling nervously as Nora's mother came out of the house.

"Oh Eli, Mama missed you so much," Nora said, setting the boy down again.

"I missed you, too, Mama. But we had a lot of fun, too. Can we go see my cousins soon? They invited me to visit." Eli cut himself off and held out his hand to Justice. "Welcome home, Pa."

Justice shook it, giving firm pressure without hurting the boy, and looked Eli in the eyes. "Thank you, son. I sure am glad to see you."

"Mother," Nora said, hugging Mrs. Taylor. "I hope everything went well for you."

"Everything went splendidly, dear. Your son was a perfect gentleman and quite a hard worker, too. I told him if you didn't look out, I was going to steal him to work my farm back in West Texas. Hello, Mr. Bullard. You are looking well. But who is this beautiful young lady accompanying you?"

"Mother, Eli," Nora said, gesturing toward Katie, who blushed at the attention. "Meet Katherine Marie Quinn, or Katie as we call her."

Katie gave a little curtsy.

Nora crouched down and put her hands on Eli's shoulders. "Eli, meet your new sister, Katie."

Eli's jaw dropped. "Sister? Really?"

Nora nodded, smiling. "Yes, really. Katie will be living with us now. We've adopted her. She's your sister."

Eli beamed at the news, looking both happy and confused then stole glances at Katie, who fairly squirmed, smiling nervously and giving him a timid wave.

"Adopted?" Mrs. Taylor said, marching forward with a warm smile. "That is wonderful news! Welcome to the family, young Katie."

Nora's mother enveloped the girl in a welcoming hug, and suddenly, Justice liked his mother-in-law very, very much.

"Eli, do you understand what we're telling you?" Nora asked.

The boy nodded, grinning from ear to ear, and latched onto his new sister's hand. "Come on, Katie! I'll teach you how to play poker!"

———

FOR A FEW DAYS, JUSTICE ENJOYED JUST BEING HOME. IT WAS nice to be back in his duds, nice to ride again, and nice to get to know Nora's mother, but most of all he enjoyed this small taste of being married to Nora, sharing a home, and being Pa to Eli and Katie.

And Katie really had become a part of the family. She worked diligently and well, helping in the house and on the ranch. She was especially good with Eli, displaying that special gift some teenage girls have for understanding the very young. Also, she had not exaggerated her love for cooking. She enjoyed helping in the kitchen, made Nora's life easier, and added some interesting twists to their meals.

One of Katie's few possessions was a bundle of recipe cards she had inherited from her mother. The cards were unnecessary now, as she had memorized all the recipes, but Katie cherished them and said she'd like to write them down someday in a proper book.

In Dos Pesos, while gearing up for the long trip to Mexico, Justice stopped at Mueller's and bought the girl a blank journal along with the few books Mueller stocked, including *Pride and Prejudice*, *Les Misérables,* and *The Count of Monte Cristo.*

"I didn't realize you were a reader, Mr. Bullard," Mueller said approvingly as he tallied the bill, "or are these for Mrs. Bullard?"

"We'll both probably read them eventually, but these are for an orphan girl we adopted."

"An orphan?" Mueller said and added two pieces of hard candy to the order. "Here's a little treat for her and one for Eli, so he doesn't feel left out. I have a soft spot for widows and orphans."

"That's very kind of you, Mr. Mueller. If you can get in more books, I'll probably buy them. This girl's a reader."

"How old is she?"

"Fifteen. But she reads like a schoolteacher. These big fat books here? She'll read each of them in a day."

"And she understands them?"

"Oh yeah, every word. You should hear Katie go on about what she reads. It's like she's living the book, not reading it."

Mueller smiled at that. "Has she read Charles Dickens?"

"I don't know."

"Well," Mueller said, reaching under the counter and coming back out with a book, "this is my personal copy of *Great Expectations.* It isn't for sale, but I've already read it several times and would be happy to lend it to her."

Justice nodded. "Thank you. I know she'll be tickled."

CHAPTER 16

Leaving the mercantile, Justice carried his purchases and the borrowed book back to the livery stable, stored them in the wagon, then went back up the street and dropped in on Clem, who was traipsing about his hotel room in that disturbing robe.

"Put on some real clothes and come down to the Third Peso for a beer," Justice said. "I'm getting ready to head to Mexico."

"In that case," the one-armed miner said, "the beer's on me. I'll be down in a jiffy."

Coming into the saloon, Justice saw Coronado sitting at a corner table, talking with one of the girls. That was a stroke of luck. It would save Justice a ride out to the Mexican's new ranch.

Justice went up to the bar, shook hands with Max Jennings, and ordered three beers.

"Thirsty?" Max joked.

Justice ambled over to Coronado, who nodded and dismissed the girl with money for a drink.

"You made it back," Coronado said, as Justice set down the beers.

"That a new hat?"

Coronado touched the spotless Stetson atop his head. "Yeah. Figured if I was going to be a gentleman farmer, I shouldn't wear a hat with bullet holes in it."

"Gotta look the part. How you doing with that? Ranching, I mean. Bossing instead of working the cattle."

Coronado drained the rest of his beer. "I'm restless as a sandstorm, *amigo*. When are we going to Mexico?"

Justice shoved one of the beers across the table to him. "Tomorrow, if it suits you."

"It suits me," Coronado said, and took a long pull off the beer.

"Garza's in Chihuahua."

"So are my people. Where in Chihuahua? It's a big place."

"Not far from Janos."

Coronado nodded. "And not far from my village. My family probably lives within thirty miles of the *hacienda*, but I have never heard of this Don Garza."

"He specializes in not being heard of."

Coronado took a drink. "Beautiful region. Good for cattle. Not so good for Apaches."

"Long way down there. I've been looking at maps. Probably five hundred miles all in, if we follow the river."

"I don't mind. Do you?"

Justice shook his head. "I'd sooner ride our horses than sit on another train anytime soon."

Coronado grinned. "You get a Pullman?"

"Oh yeah. Only the finest."

"I hear rich people have a restaurant on the long-haul train."

"You hear right."

"Good food?"

"Like a dream."

"You had your fill, though?"

Justice nodded.

Coronado touched his new hat again. "I hate this hat. I'm going to wear my old hat to Mexico."

"Don't," Justice chuckled. "This is your chance to break it in."

"You're right, *amigo*. In fact, between the Apaches, *bandidos*, and *rurales*, I might even get a new bullet hole."

"Not to mention Garza's men. One of them is pretty good, I hear."

"I'll bring my rifle, then," Garza said with a crafty smile. "We'll shoot him first. From about three hundred yards away."

When Clem arrived, Justice pulled the map from his pocket and spread it out on the table. They weighed down the edges with their beers and Justice dragged a finger along the Rio Grande all the way to El Paso then traced the road south into Mexico.

Coronado shook his head. "Too far east. Too many *rurales* and *bandidos* on that road. Besides, my people are here." He stabbed the map between two large lakes in the mountains far to the west of El Paso.

"That's Apache country."

Coronado smiled. "My father rode with Goyahkla."

"Geronimo?"

Coronado nodded.

Clem shook his head. "Here I am, associating with a gunman and an Apache. I gotta rethink my associations."

Ignoring his white-bearded friend, Justice asked Coronado, "You are Chiricahua?"

Coronado shook his head. "No, but the Spanish persecuted more people than just the Chiricahua. My father didn't so much ride with the Apaches as ride against the Spanish."

"Makes sense."

"The land is beautiful but violent. It is how we live there. Trade one day, kill the next. But I do not think violence concerns you much."

"Not especially," Justice said. "So how do we get there?"

"We follow the river until we get about thirty miles below Las Palomas. Then we head southwest on the wagon trail that runs from Hatch to Deming."

"Dry country to be leaving the river," Clem said.

"I know where to find water," Coronado said. He traced the route on the map then pushed his finger over the border and into the desert beyond. "This is hard country, but we will meet fewer *rurales* and *bandidos*. Also, many of the Apaches are gone now. Either to the reservation or raiding in Arizona and the valley of *Río Sonora*."

"I heard General Crook caught up to Geronimo last spring," Clem said.

"I heard the same thing," Coronado said. "The Mexican government allowed US forces to cross the border. Geronimo was surprised and disheartened to learn how Crook found him."

"Apache scouts," Justice said.

Coronado nodded. "It was a knife in the back to Geronimo and his people. When you consider the history of Chihuahua, all the violence, all the massacres, it was as bitter and surprising to Geronimo as it would be to you if Nora betrayed you to Garza."

Clem scratched his beard. "Sounds like you boys are riding into a slaughterhouse down there."

"Things are quieter now than they were a few years ago, but yes, there are many ways to die in that land." Coronado smiled. "It will be good to see my home again."

CHAPTER 17

The next morning, the weather was perfect for riding. Bright and sunny and cool with a slight breeze at their backs.

Justice and Coronado took the river road and headed south, the Mexican clearly ready for a break from his new life of leisure.

They packed as light as they could, which didn't end up being very light. They favored weapons and ammunition over provisions, figuring they could eat at *cantinas* and *restaurantes* along the river. Then, before heading into the mountainous southwestern borderlands, they could buy pack horses and panniers along with enough supplies to see them through to Coronado's village.

Justice took a Winchester, the 8 gauge, his custom Colts in their double holster, and the Webley and Bowie knife in their shoulder rig, along with plenty of ammunition and six sticks of dynamite from the crate Matt had given him.

He handed another half dozen sticks to Coronado. "We end up needing to make some noise, there is no substitute for dynamite."

Coronado grinned. "I remember the raid on Tucker's ranch. I think maybe you like blowing things up."

"There is that, too."

They made good time, riding out of the mountains, heading steadily downhill. As they descended, the sun rose, and by noon, the day had warmed considerably.

They rested their horses, letting them drink their fill and forage on the heavy grass of the riverbank.

Dagger seemed happy to be off the ranch and stretching his muscular legs.

"That is quite a horse," Coronado said. "He will make you a target, you know."

"I'm always a target. I might as well ride a good horse."

"Well, when trouble comes, just don't go speeding off on your racehorse and leave your friend Coronado in the thick of it."

They made thirty miles that day and stopped at the San Ildefonso Pueblo Reservation, where the small community, despite their obvious poverty, insisted on feeding them and caring for their horses. They invited Justice and Coronado to sleep in the church, which was nice, given the chill of the night.

The next morning, Justice thanked the villagers and gave the elders ten dollars in greenbacks and a sack of Arbuckles.

When they hit the trail again, Coronado said, "We run out of coffee, you're gonna regret that, amigo."

Justice shrugged. "I reckon we'll get a chance to resupply before they do."

The country around them grew drier, but the river provided all the water they needed. They rode through a magnificent canyon. Its steep, sagebrush-studded walls rose a thousand feet in the air.

Both men stayed alert for bandits who might be lying in wait, but they had no trouble. One evening, they caught catfish and had them for dinner. Beside the campfire, Coronado told the old stories of the beginning of the world, when Apaches were monster killers. Then they bedded down beneath the stars, trusting their horses to alert them if any threat approached.

Late in the afternoon of the second day after leaving San Ildefonso, they arrived at Bernalillo, where they left their horses at the livery, restocked their coffee and provisions, and booked rooms in a little *posada* at the center of town.

They had a supper of shredded beef *enchiladas* and *tamales*. Each man washed down the wonderful food with a few *cervezas*.

Coronado touched his hat, which didn't look quite so new anymore. "My time as a wealthy rancher has weakened me, *amigo*. I am looking forward to sleeping in a real bed tonight."

"That's not weakness, that's common sense," Justice said. "This food's good enough for me to stay in town for a couple of days. What do you say?"

"The hostler seemed good. We could give the horses a rest. Long road ahead."

It was decided, then. After supper, they moseyed back to the hotel and paid for another night.

They loafed the next day, spending time at the *restaurante*, visiting their horses, and hiring baths at the barber. It felt good to be clean.

The next day, they stopped at midday in Albuquerque, a pleasant, well-to-do town that was on the rise, thanks to the Atchison, Topeka, and Santa Fe line coming through three years earlier and setting up its railyards and passenger depot just two miles to the east.

A few thousand people called Albuquerque home. The shops and streets were neat, and with folks building everywhere, the air fairly crackled with excitement. You could feel the impending growth and progress in Albuquerque the way you could detect a hint of spring in the breeze some late-winter days.

They took their dinner in a *cantina* at the edge of town. The *posole* was thick and delicious with few spices, preserving the flavor of the fatty pork and the sweet nutti-ness of the hominy.

They were tempted to stay but didn't want to lose half a day of travel, so they got on the road again and that evening camped along the river a couple of miles north of Peralta, where Confederates had gotten chased off toward the end of Sibley's New Mexico campaign.

Having heard rumors of Apaches, the men slept in shifts. Justice took first watch and spent it fending off thoughts of home while he kept his eyes peeled and his ears open. Staying awake wouldn't have been a problem even without the threat of Apaches, thanks to the frigid nighttime temper-ature. In the morning, a thin layer of ice had formed at the river's edge.

They headed south and two days later arrived in another rail town, Socorro. They boarded their horses at the livery and walked the main street, which boasted brick buildings and telegraph lines.

Justice pointed at a sign hanging from the awning in front of a large brick building. "Candy, ice cream, soda. My boy would like that. Katie, too, I reckon."

"That gives me an idea," Coronado said, and walked into the store.

Watching Coronado make his purchases, Justice grinned. Then he discovered a rack of books for sale and purchased half a dozen.

"You gonna carry those all the way to Mexico and back?" Coronado asked. "How will you keep them dry during river crossings?"

"I'm not lugging them with us. Come on. Let's find the post office. I want to send some telegrams, too."

The books cost nearly four dollars to ship. It was a fortune, but Justice didn't hesitate, including a quick note to Nora and a stick of hard candy for each of the children. On the inside cover of *Alice's Adventures in Wonderland*, he inscribed, *Katie, I hope these books will help you feel at home because that's where you are now. Love, Pa.*

The telegraph station was right next to the post office. He fired off two telegrams, one to his wife, the other to his brother.

NORA BULLARD, DOS PESOS (STOP) MADE IT TO SOCORRO (stop) No trouble so far (stop) Love and miss you terribly (stop) My best to the children (stop) Justice

TO MATT, HE WROTE:

MATT BULLARD, FREDERICKSBURG, TX (STOP) IN SOCORRO (stop) On way to Janos (stop) D.G. hacienda near there (stop) Give Luke a hard time (stop) I believe he's in love (stop) Hope you're healing up (stop) Jake

THEY RENTED ROOMS IN THE *POSADA*, SLEPT WELL, AND BROKE their fast with Mexican oatmeal. It was sweet and warm and filling with bits of soft apple cooked in.

Justice paid the bill, left a nice tip, and purchased two apples, which he quartered outside the *restaurante*.

Half of these he handed to Coronado. "A meal like that makes me think the horses should have something nice, too."

"You have a reputation as a killer," Coronado said as they headed for the livery. "I don't know if I would have made this trip if I had known you were so sentimental."

"So says the man with a saddlebag full of hard candy."

Coronado laughed. "This candy will make me a hero to the children in my village. And these," he said, holding up the cigars he had purchased, "will perhaps help my *abuela* to forgive my long absence. My grandmother loves a fine cigar."

CHAPTER 18

Justice spotted a feather of dust lifting into the windless morning from atop the ridge to their right.

He didn't have to say anything to Coronado. Men such as they, conditioned to travel through hard country, were as attuned to changes in their environment as the nose of a hound is attuned to fresh scent on dry ground.

Leaving the trail, the men rode into the trees near the river, which was broad and slow-moving here.

Stealing a quick glance toward the ridge and spotting more dust, Justice pulled his rifle from its boot.

"Fight, then?" Coronado asked.

Justice nodded, dismounting. "It's time to rest the horses anyway. Besides, if they're Apaches, they might be showing us their dust and trying to chase us into an ambush."

After leaving Socorro, they had slept under the stars for two nights. They had been traveling easily, and the horses were holding up well. Now only a few hours' ride outside of Las Palomas, they had been on the lookout for Apaches, having heard of a teamster who had been knifed in the livery of that small town.

Not wanting their pursuers to know they had spotted them, they pretended to be stopping merely to rest the horses.

Meanwhile, Justice scanned the terrain. "Hitch them by the water, right here where the trees are thickest. I'll get down behind that fallen tree. You get in behind that boulder."

Coronado hitched his horse without a word, fetched his canteen, and shouldered his saddlebags.

Justice did the same. Seventy yards to their west, a larger plume lifted a hundred feet up a loose embankment of stone and dirt, sand and scrub.

Without any further conversation, Justice and Coronado parted, walking calmly but keeping an eye on the ridge.

When Justice was ten feet from the fallen tree, he saw what he'd been expecting: a glint of metal from up on the ridge.

He sprinted forward and dove to the ground, mindful of his muzzle, just as the first gunshot cracked from up above.

A burst of shots followed, three or four rifles firing down at them. Bullets cut the air above Justice's head and walloped into the heavy trunk of the huge tree behind which he'd taken shelter. It was an ancient oak, a massive timber that had fallen somewhere far upstream and been carried many miles by some springtime flood and deposited here upon this slope as if for the sole purpose of protecting him in this moment.

And protect him it did.

He glanced in Coronado's direction and saw his friend crouched safely behind the boulder.

After several seconds, the shooting stopped. As the echoes faded, Justice risked a quick glance.

Rifles exploded above, firing another volley into his position.

But he had revealed himself for only a fraction of a second, just long enough to note their positions.

He'd seen rifles beneath the outline of three sombreros. They were spaced only a few feet apart.

There could be others, of course, but given the sloppy attack and tight spacing of the men, Justice doubted it. This felt like the shoddy work of occasional bandits.

"*Señores*," a deep voice called down from above. "*Por que nos atacaste?*"

Justice laughed loudly and responded in Spanish, "We did not attack you... yet."

"We do not want trouble," the man hollered down in his native tongue, and his voice was gravelly with suppressed laughter. "We are merely frightened farmers, trying to protect our lives. Show yourselves so we know you mean us no harm, and we will continue on our way."

"Do you promise not to shoot?" Justice asked. Taking off his hat, he glanced toward Coronado.

Coronado watched Justice place his hat on his rifle then nodded, knowing what Justice was going to do.

"Yes, we promise, my friend," the bandit called down.

"All right," Justice replied in a tentative voice. "I'm standing up. Now don't you shoot me."

He lifted his hat into view, and the bandits opened fire.

Coronado popped up and fired rapidly, worked his lever, and fired again.

Up above men cried out.

Justice was already moving. The bandits had knocked his hat from his rifle. He low crawled down the trunk ten feet, popped up, and fired at the ridge.

He saw no bandits, save for the limp form of a man draped over the summit, but he hammered their position, keeping them on the defensive.

Coronado took advantage of the opportunity, jumped up,

and ran forward, crossing the road and hiding himself behind a pile of sandy talus at the base of the ridge.

When his friend was safe, Justice slipped behind the tree and reloaded. Up on the ridge, a single rifle fired down at him.

Staying low, Justice worked his way farther down the tree toward the great tangle of its wild roots.

The firing stopped from above. From his position, Justice could see Coronado rushing up the bank toward a lower ridge.

Justice rose and fired three times, giving his friend cover.

There was no return fire. Justice stayed in position, rifle at the ready, scanning back and forth, ready for any movement.

Following the fold of the land, Coronado worked his way up the embankment and topped the ridge eighty yards to the north of the bandits' original position.

"He's running for it," Coronado shouted down. "Riding south, angling toward the road. The others are dead."

Justice ran back to the river, untethered his horse, and sheathed his rifle. Pulling a Colt, he mounted up. "All right, Dagger. Let's see what you can do."

He charged after the bandit, pounding full speed down the road. It was dangerous, he knew, but not half so dangerous as allowing the man to get out in front of them.

Right now, the bandit had given in to his natural cowardice. His partners were dead. He was wild with fear, desperate to escape.

This was the time to destroy an enemy, Justice knew, immediately after you shattered his line and he broke ranks and fled. Whether in a battle, a fist fight, or a moment like this, you kept rolling until it was over.

He leaned across Dagger, urging the stallion forward, and

the horse devoured the road, hooves pounding, flying ahead faster than Justice had ever ridden.

A moment later, the bandit appeared, slapping his horse for all it was worth.

Which wasn't much, given the way Dagger ate its wake.

When Justice drew to within twenty yards, he eased his pace and concentrated his aim.

Sensing him, the bandit turned in his saddle and fired wildly.

Justice squeezed the trigger—once, twice, three times—then turned Dagger sharply to the left and urged him into a full gallop.

This forced the bandit to adjust. He twisted, trying to bring his pistol across his body.

Having pulled within ten feet, Justice fired.

The bandit jerked, hit hard, low in the side, and Justice fired again.

This round punched through the bandit's armpit and knocked him out of his saddle. He was dead before he hit the scrub brush.

Justice reloaded and headed back toward Coronado, who met him in the middle.

"You get him?"

Justice nodded. "Anyone else back there?"

"Just the dead. What do we do with them?"

"Leave them for the buzzards. They chose this, not us."

Justice searched the man he'd killed and took his gun and ammunition and the few pesos on his person then dragged him off the road, hid him in a sandy ditch, and covered him over with brush.

It wouldn't keep the scavengers away, but it would keep riders from spotting the dead man until they had cleared out of the country.

They caught the bandit's horse and after a short discussion, decided to dump the saddle and cut the animal free, figuring these bandits as locals who might have friends on the trail ahead.

"Guess this means a change of plans," Coronado said.

Justice nodded. "I was looking forward to sleeping in the *posada* in Las Palomas and giving the horses a rest, but I reckon we'll just stop for dinner, ride on toward Hatch, and camp ten or fifteen miles down the road. This is some country."

Coronado grinned. "Oh yeah. But just wait till we get to Mexico, my friend."

CHAPTER 19

The next day, they rode into Hatch. It was early afternoon. Having come farther than originally planned the previous day, they only rode twenty miles that morning, starting early and resting the horses twice along the way.

Miguel Torres, the old hostler who took their horses, led them from the stable to his home, which served as the small town's *posada, restaurante,* and *cantina*, and introduced them to his wife, a kindly old woman that Justice and Coronado showed all due respect.

They rented two small rooms then took turns getting cleaned up.

While Coronado bathed, Justice bought a *cerveza*. He was surprised to find beer here, but Mrs. Torres explained with a smile that people here grew the best chiles in the world, so beer was necessary.

Justice thanked her and went back out to talk with her husband.

"You folks have much trouble with Apaches?"

"Now? No, not so much," Mr. Torres said. "But Trouble with Apaches could be the name of this town."

Mr. Torres had helped found the little farming town in 1851.

"It was called Santa Barbara first," he explained. "We had problems with Apaches from the beginning. They drove us out, and we didn't come back until 1853, when Fort Thorn opened."

He shook his head. "It wasn't much of a fort, but it helped. Then in '59, Fort Thorn closed, and the Apaches drove us out again the next year. I moved to Las Palomas and didn't come back for fifteen years. By then, the worst of the Indian trouble was over. We renamed our town Hatch."

"In honor of General Hatch?" Justice asked between sips.

Torres nodded. "Great Indian fighter."

"So where are the Apaches now?"

Torres spread his hands. "Where is the wind?"

Justice nodded. "We're heading to Deming then on down into Mexico. What do you hear about things down that way?"

"From here to Deming, you should have no trouble. Well, maybe you will, maybe you won't, but beyond that? The borderlands are full of *bandidos* and Apaches, *señor.*"

"So I've heard."

After Coronado emerged wearing a new shirt and carrying a beer, Justice took his leave and got cleaned up. He shaved and bathed and emerged feeling human again, then put on his clean clothes and hired Mrs. Torres to launder his and Coronado's trail duds.

For supper, Mrs. Torres prepared a comforting meal: *sopapillas* and honey alongside a spicy stew with thick chunks of pork and potato and loaded with onions, carrots, and the best green chiles Justice had ever tasted.

They ate family style together with the Torreses at their

table, bowing their heads as Mr. Torres said the blessing, wishing them safe travels and water on their journey, then diving into their meals with gusto, accepting extra servings from the ladle of the smiling Mrs. Torres, sopping up the last of their bowls with their remaining *sopapillas*, and washing it all down with more *cerveza*.

"Ma'am," Justice said, when they finished, "that was the best meal I've had in a long time. Thank you so much."

Coronado nodded, adding his appreciation.

Mrs. Torres gave a slight bow of her head. "*Gracias, señores.* It gives me great pleasure to see you enjoy the food."

"Someday," Mr. Torres said, "Hatch will be famous. Not for its trouble with the Apaches but for its peppers."

They turned in early and woke early then enjoyed a pot of steaming coffee and a breakfast of scrambled eggs and fried potatoes, both dishes prepared with fried onions and green chiles.

All in, their bill came to a modest four dollars and fifty cents.

Justice handed the Torreses seven dollars and again expressed his gratitude.

"Thank you, señor," Mr. and Mrs. Torres chorused. "Please visit us again. *Vaya con Dios.*"

From Hatch, they left the river and passed into a dry land of red hills and mesas with occasional stands of poplar and scrub brush and mesquite everywhere.

Good to his word, Coronado knew where to find water and near one of these streams, the Mexican grinned and asked Justice if he wanted to see something amazing.

"What is it?"

"Better to see than to hear, *amigo.* Come. Let the horses drink and rest."

Justice shrugged and followed Coronado off the trail. Deming was 48 miles from Hatch, a comfortable two-day trip on seasoned trail horses but too much to cover in a single day unless you wanted to rest your horse for a few days afterward, so they had extra time.

Coronado scrambled over the loose red soil, scaling the mesa. Halfway up, they reached a cliff of stone and followed a narrow trail to a patch of scrub that screened a cave near the top.

Coronado grinned and Justice understood that his friend had been looking forward to this surprise. The Mexican withdrew a candle and matches, lit the candle, and entered the cave. "Come, *amigo*, let me show you something special that I discovered years ago seeking shelter from a storm."

Inside, Coronado swung his arm, sweeping the candle-light over an amazing sight.

A stone ledge had been chiseled from the wall. Atop this ledge rested dozens of perfect bowls.

"The old people made these," Coronado explained, leaning close so Justice could see the bold geometric patterns within the black-and-white pottery, "hundreds of years before the Spanish arrived."

Neither man spoke for a time, taking in this glimpse of ancient times with reverent silence, each man moved in ways and by forces he could not understand.

When they emerged from the cave, they squinted, the day seeming brighter and hotter than it had, and Justice felt he knew his companion better somehow.

Coronado had carried one of the bowls out of the cave. As he wrapped the artifact in his spare shirt and stored it with great care in his saddle bag, he explained that he had never taken anything before and never would again. "This is for my *abuela*. She has made pottery her whole life. She is very interested in this place but is too old to make the trip from Mexico."

That afternoon, they rode halfway to Deming and

camped beside a spring sheltered by a shelf of rock and surrounded by a stand of tall poplars.

Mindful of Apaches, they went without a fire and slept in shifts.

Coronado took first watch and had nothing to report when he spoke to Justice, waking him from dreams of home.

Justice stood watch with the 8 gauge in hand, missing Nora and Eli. He wondered how they were getting along with Katie. Fine, he supposed.

Had Mrs. Taylor left yet? Likely so.

Had Faith and Luke made plans to see each other again? It was quite a span between Fredericksburg and West Texas, but young love had a way of treating miles like inches, and he didn't reckon Luke and Faith would let distance keep them apart.

What if they stuck? What if they got married?

If that happened, Mrs. Taylor would have to decide what she was going to do and where she was going to live. She certainly wouldn't live alone on a ranch in West Texas.

If she chose to live in Fredericksburg or Dos Pesos, Justice would offer to build her a house. It was the least he could do for the woman who had birthed and raised the love of his life.

Then a funny thought occurred to him. If the pair did get married, Luke would be his cousin and his brother-in-law.

He grinned—and then heard Dagger snort with concern.

Moving quietly in that direction, he spotted a long form slipping slowly and silently through the moonlight thirty yards from the horses.

He raised the scattergun, ready to pull the trigger but not wanting to alert every Apache for miles.

"Get out of here, cat."

The mountain lion snarled, turning in his direction and hunching low, its ears pinned back.

Holding the shotgun steady, Justice stomped the ground. "Get out now."

Muscle rippled beneath the cat's tawny coat as its hind quarters rose and its tail lashed liquidly back and forth.

Justice knew this could go either way. Since the cat was close to forty yards from him, he gambled and crouched and picked up a rock, keeping the barrel trained on the snarling lion the whole time.

When he stood, the lion gave a horrible, squalling scream that made the hairs at the back of Justice's neck snap to attention.

Surreptitiously, the mountain lion swiveled closer, trying to get in range to pounce.

Justice took aim and hurled the rock, which nailed the thing in the shoulder.

With another wild squeal the cat leapt.

Justice was a fraction of a second from blowing it away when he realized that the animal had not leapt at him but ten feet straight into the air.

It landed with the curious grace of cats everywhere and shot away into the brush moving away from him and his horses as fast as it could travel.

Listening to its retreat, Justice thought, *I'm glad I didn't have to kill you, cat.*

CHAPTER 20

"Welcome to New Chicago," the clerk said when they entered the Transcontinental Hotel in Deming. "You men need a room?"

"Two rooms," Justice said. "He snores."

The clerk gave a genuine laugh and got them all set up, chattering amiably the whole time, building up this fledgling town in grandiose terms.

"Yes sir," the clerk said, "they don't call it New Chicago for nothing. They drove the Silver Spike two years ago, completing the nation's second transcontinental railroad. Yes sir, that's right. You hop a train here and you can ride all the way to California or New York, whichever you please."

"You got a line to Janos, Chihuahua?" Coronado joked.

The clerk took him seriously. "No sir, but you hang around here a while I can all but guarantee we will. I'm telling you, Deming is the next Chicago, the future of New Mexico!"

Deming wasn't half as big as you would have guessed, based on the gushing clerk's exuberance, but it was big enough to support several restaurants and four saloons and had a sizeable mercantile, where they resupplied prior to heading out for supper and maybe a few cold *cervezas* after.

From the hostler with whom they'd left their horses, they had purchased a pack horse and a pack saddle. Now they bought extra water skins, panniers, and more supplies than they reckoned they would need in Mexico, along with some farming tools, medical supplies, scented soap, and fabric Coronado thought his family might appreciate.

They hauled all this back to their rooms, glad they'd made it to town in time to take care of business. That way, they could get started early.

They were only thirty-five miles from Mexico and around a hundred from Coronado's village.

Justice sure hoped he'd find Garza and Rose at the *hacienda*. He hadn't come all this way just to see the sights and sample the food. He aimed to bring down the head of this international crime organization, kill the man who'd shot his pa, save countless girls trapped in the worst way on the wrong side of the border, and give himself a fighting chance at earning a marriage exemption from the Commander of the silent justices.

Justice and Coronado both loved Mexican food, but when they discovered a restaurant run by Mennonites, they ambled in, ready to shake things up.

It ended up being a great choice. Dinner started with two-layered *zwieback* rolls, which they dipped in a tureen of melted *queso Menonita*, which Coronado explained had originated with the Mennonites who fled into Chihuahua fearing religious persecution.

Next came bowls of sweet, dark red *borscht*, which Justice loved. The only thing that would have made it better would've been a cold beer. Entering the restaurant, he had hoped to find something rivaling the German beers in Fredericksburg, but he was plum out of luck, because the Mennonites were teetotalers across the board.

Supper almost made up for their lack of spirits. They poured white gravy over bowls of smoked sausage chopped up with boiled potatoes and cabbage.

Without even asking, the waitress brought out rice pudding for dessert. Justice felt duty-bound to finish every bite, and by the time he paid and waddled out, he felt like a one-gallon skin packing two gallons of water.

That being said, when Coronado suggested getting a beer at one of the saloons, Justice couldn't say no. After all, this might be their last beer in a long time.

They walked into the Silver Spike. There was a pretty good crowd of people inside and by their makeup—at a glance, Justice spotted cowboys, businessmen, drummers, gamblers, travelers, and, of course, saloon girls—this could have been any saloon in any rail town in the West.

Only as they made their way to the bar, he picked up a couple of differences between the Silver Spike and run-of-the-mill saloons.

First, whoever owned this place was doubling down on the same enthusiasm expressed by the hotel clerk. Train-themed art adorned the walls, and the bar itself was a raft of bound railroad ties set atop barrels.

The bartender wore a little conductor's cap, and a sign over the sparkling liquor shelf read, *Welcome to New Chicago.*

Deming was clearly a town determined to make something of itself.

The other significant difference between the Silver Spike and other saloons was the beauty of its working girls. Justice had no interest in these women, of course, but you would have to be blind not to notice their beauty.

The girls were of a type: young, slender, and girlish with long, raven-black hair and big, dark eyes, as if a single-minded recruiter had searched all the villages of northern Mexico and selected only the most beautiful young women who fit his tastes exactly.

Their supervisor could have been their mother. She was beautiful and elegant, though Justice did not miss the hardness of her eyes, which twinkled like chips of volcanic stone. She looked more like the *dama* of a stately *hacienda* than a madame in a rail town bordello.

They got beers and took the only open table, sitting against the wall near an open door through which Justice could see a set of steps leading upstairs. Over the door, a small sign read, *Pleasure Depot*.

They sipped the beers, letting the big meal settle, neither man feeling the need to speak. Justice watched people come and go.

Half of these folks were just passing through.

One of the locals, a weasel-faced man with a thin mustache and a dark bowler hat, was cheating at poker. The travelers at the table clearly had no idea.

One of the drunken cowboys across the room, a young guy with a curly tangle of greasy hair and the shadow of a black eye fading on his face, was growing louder and more agitated, looking for a fight, which meant he had probably lost his last scrap.

The broad-shouldered, well-dressed man in the corner was the saloon minder. He wore a Colt on his hip. A short cudgel leaned against the wall beside him. From time to time, he made eye contact with a burly man sitting at the far end of the bar.

This man also wore a pistol but had the air of a supervisor, not a bouncer. The bartender drifted his way occasionally, and once, the elegant madame came over and spoke to him.

Justice figured he was the boss man, then.

"Another round?" Coronado asked, finishing his beer.

"Yeah, I could drink another."

Coronado rose and headed for the bar.

A moment later, one of the working girls came over to Justice.

"*Hola, señor.*"

"*Hola, señorita.*"

She laid a tiny hand on his shoulder and smiled prettily down at him, though it wasn't hard to see how forced her smile was. "Would you like company this night?" she asked, struggling with the English.

"No thank you," he said, and held up his hand so she could see the golden wedding band.

She smiled at the ring. "I no tell if you no tell, *señor*," she said, her smile more strained than ever.

The poor girl. Up close, he could see she was only a couple of years older than Katie. What was she doing here?

He shook his head. "Not interested," he told her in Spanish. "You take good care, miss."

She gave a little curtsy and was about to leave when Coronado showed up and stared at the girl with shock. "Isabela! What are you doing here?"

CHAPTER 21

The girl's face convulsed through a series of rapid-fire changes, registering shock and recognition, excitement and shame and something strange… hope?

"*Primo,*" she wept. "I am sorry."

"Sorry? What did you do?"

"Nothing. Everything. I am so ashamed." She started to turn away, but Coronado set down the beers and brought her back to the table.

Justice noticed the minder was staring in their direction now.

"I don't understand," Coronado said. "Why aren't you home in the village? What are you doing here, of all places? You're just a girl, Isabela."

It was too much for her. She broke down sobbing and couldn't speak.

Justice heard this but didn't see it because he was scanning the bar and getting a bad feeling.

The burly man at the bar had turned now and was staring at them with a wary, calculating look. He disguised the move well, but Justice saw the man swipe a hand across his hip and unfasten the hammer loop atop his six-shooter.

"Tell me," Coronado said, anger creeping into his voice. "Who brought you here? Was it Roderigo?"

"No," Isabela wept. "No, no, no."

The man at the bar nodded at the minder, who stood and picked up the cudgel, holding it against his leg.

"Who then?" Coronado demanded.

"Please leave, *Primo*. You will get me in big trouble."

"I'm leaving, all right, but I'm taking you with me. You are going back to your mother, Isabela."

"No," Isabela said, her voice sharp with terror now. "They will kill you if you try."

The minder crept closer, covering half the distance to their table and feigning interest in the card game.

The madame went over to the man at the bar, who spoke to her. She nodded and came their way, smiling beneath those glittering obsidian eyes.

Snake's eyes, Justice thought. *This woman has the eyes of a deadly viper.*

He shoved his chair back a little, angling himself toward the woman but pretending not to notice her. His eyes swept over the room but found no additional threats.

"Kill me? I don't think so, *Primita*. Now tell me why you are here."

"Men came to the village after you left. Bad men. They took me away. Ricardo tried to stop them, but they—"

"Good evening, gentlemen," the viper woman said, drawing near.

Justice used her arrival as an excuse to stand. He nodded slightly and tipped his hat. "Ma'am."

She smiled but beneath her sugary smile, her voice was razor-sharp steel. "Isabela, dear. *Señor* Painter wishes to speak with you at the bar. Now."

Isabela dipped her head like a dog used to the boot.

And just like that, the killing frost settled over Justice.

The man at the bar—presumably Mr. Painter—had swiveled around to face them now, and the minder came across the floor, heading toward the wall, trying to get behind Justice, the cudgel still held low at his side.

"Yes, *Señora* Flores," Isabela said meekly.

"She's not going anywhere," Coronado declared. "Who's in charge here?"

"I am," the woman declared icily, and just like that, she had a derringer pointed at Coronado's face. "And you are leaving."

"*Señora*, please," Isabela begged. "These men are drunk. They will leave."

The minder rushed forward.

With one lightning-quick twitch, Justice filled his hands with iron, drawing back the hammers with audible clicks as he leveled one on the minder and pressed the other into the back of *Señora* Flores's skull.

"Put down your pocket pistol," he demanded, "and you, stand right where you are."

Both people complied instantly.

Coronado took the madame's pistol and drew his own.

Justice took two steps back, opening his field of view, keeping an eye on Painter, who was hadn't drawn but was speaking to the bartender, whose ridiculous little conductor's hat had gone askew above his startled features.

"Bar dog, you keep your hands where I can see them," Justice said, his voice loud but steady, full of command. "You reach under there a shotgun, I will shoot you right between the eyes."

All around the bar, patrons reacted. Most froze, but several chairs scraped at once, frightened drummers bolting for the door.

Painter used this distraction, drawing his revolver behind the screen of scurrying men.

Justice dropped into a half-crouch, arms akimbo, as the minder dropped his cudgel and went for his six-shooter.

Justice shot him in the chest.

The minder stumbled backward, fired into the ceiling, and dropped.

Around the room, folks hollered and jumped up, overturning tables, running for cover, and drawing their own weapons.

Painter's pistol boomed, and someone between Justice and the bar cried out and fell to the floor, opening a space between him and the murderous Painter, who fired again, smashing a bullet into the wall above Justice's head.

Justice fired three times in rapid succession, not wanting to hit any of the innocent folks darting across the room.

The first shot went wide and smashed the fancy mirror behind the bar. The second grazed Painter's face, slicing across his cheek. The third hit him right in the teeth.

The bartender stood there, scared out of his wits, with his hands high in the air. Around the room, several men pointed pistols toward Justice and Coronado. These were not Painter's men, Justice saw. But they could kill him just as dead. Their expressions were confused and wary. If one of them fired, they all would.

"Don't shoot!" Isabela cried. "These men are good men. They are saving me. I was stolen, brought here, made to work! This man is my cousin."

"Don't listen to her," *Señora* Flores said coolly. "Disarm these murderers and fetch the marshal. This girl is afraid. She is lying."

"No, she isn't lying," another girl spoke up. "We were all kidnapped and brought here against our will."

"It is true," another girl said, and pointed to the dead men.

"These men stole us from our homes and forced us into prostitution." She turned angry eyes on the madame. "And so did *Señora* Flores!"

All around the room, pistols lowered.

"All you poor girls, come with us now," Justice said. "We're getting you out of here."

The girls didn't hesitate. They rushed forward, desperate to escape this nightmare. To the men, Justice said, "I don't want to kill this Flores woman, but I don't want her running for help. Will someone keep her here until we get out of town?"

"I will," a man said, stepping forward.

"Me too," another man said.

"We'll lend a hand, too," the belligerent cowboy said, focusing his aggression on this new task. "Me and the boys will give you an escort out of town. Ain't that right, boys?"

His seven dusty companions nodded.

"I appreciate that, everyone," Justice said. "Girls, are we forgetting anyone?"

"Sylvia is still upstairs," one of the young women said.

"So is Elena," another added.

"How are we gonna get them all out of here?" Coronado asked.

"There is a stable in back," Isabela said. "Painter has a wagon and horses."

"Stealing!" Mrs. Flores hissed. "You ungrateful thief!"

Isabela lashed out, slapping the elegant woman hard across the face. "You are the devil! I ought to claw your eyes out!"

Coronado stepped between them and shoved Flores into the grip of a scowling man.

A minute later, the girls returned from upstairs with two other women still tugging their clothes around them.

"Let's go, everyone," Justice said. He had reloaded and

returned one Colt to its holster. Now he moved toward the door. "First, the hotel. Then the livery. Then we ride."

"Come on, boys!" the bruised cowboy hooted. "Anybody tries to stop these folks, we'll kill him deader than a hammer!"

CHAPTER 22

The cowboys were good to their word. They didn't end
up having to shoot anyone, but they did provide secu-
rity for the seven young women while Justice and Coronado
gathered their things, got their horses saddled and loaded,
and settled the bill with the hostler, who was full of
questions.

Justice told the man the truth. Well, he at least told him
about the Silver Spike, what had been going on there, and
how they had set these poor women free. He did not
mention Don Garza, not wanting the man to have any
inkling that he was coming for him.

Someone had indeed gone to fetch the marshal, but
Justice never saw the man. The marshal was stopped by an
outraged crowd in front of the Silver Spike. From what
Justice heard, the men and women gathered there were ready
to string up *Señora* Flores and the terrified bartender as well.
The marshal, who was no doubt paid off by Garza's people,
had his hands too full with keeping that from happening to
come the rest of the way down the street and get himself
killed trying to apprehend Justice.

The cowboys, who appeared to consider defending these young women as a matter of chivalry, escorted them out of Deming and rode with them for a few miles before turning back to guard the road against any posse the marshal might send after them.

The night was cold but bright, thanks to the huge moon shining down from the cloudless sky. By its light, they traveled through the night.

The women huddled in the wagon beneath the hay and saddle blankets Justice had purchased from the hostler. Some of the girls wept. Some laughed, rejoicing. Some whispered incessantly. Some stared into the darkness, lost in their own thoughts.

When they broke for camp at dawn, they had covered half the distance to Mexico. They pulled off the road onto a faint trail that led to a clearing where an adobe house sat long abandoned.

"This will get us off the main road, anyway," Justice said, "and if we have to make a stand, we will at least have the house."

As he and Coronado tended to the horses, Isabela and one of the more talkative girls went inside the house and found a broom and swept the floor and cleared away spiderwebs, then checked the place by candlelight for snakes and scorpions.

Once the house was cleared, the girls bedded down inside.

Justice volunteered for first watch. Coronado accepted but stayed awake first to talk.

"Think this is Garza's work?" Coronado asked.

"I'm sure it is."

"The girls tell you?"

"No, but one of them was taken to a grand *hacienda* near Janos. The *Don* there made her one of his women for a short time. She never knew his name, but I guarantee it was Garza. Apparently, he had a small army of guards, including a man who sounds a lot like Rose, and a whole harem of kidnapped girls. But this girl—Ines, I think is her name—she wouldn't cavort for him, so he shipped her over the border."

"Lucky for her."

"You can say that again, partner. I can't imagine what these poor girls have been through."

"I don't even want to think about it. I've known my *prima* since the day she was born. I held her in my hands. I am going to kill *Don* Garza."

"Get in line, buddy."

"A competition between friends, then," Coronado said. "We will see who kills him. What are the stakes, huh? A beer?"

"Sounds good. I always enjoy a free beer."

"We will see who enjoys a free beer, *amigo*. But first, we must return these poor girls to their homes."

"Yeah, about that," Justice said. He'd spent a lot of time working this over in his head as they'd traveled through the night. "They can't go home yet."

"Why, because of Garza?"

Justice nodded. "Sometime this morning, he'll know we stole his girls. Garza isn't stupid. He'll ask questions. Who we were, what we looked like, what we said."

Coronado shook his head. "Kind of wish we'd shot that Flores woman."

"We would've been doing the world a service, but I'm not the man for that kind of work, and I don't think you are, either."

"No, but I still wish she was dead."

"She might be, given how angry that mob was. But we have to assume she survived and will be sending Garza a telegram first thing this morning."

"They'll probably figure out we're headed this way."

"They'd be stupid if they didn't."

"You think Garza will send someone to intercept us?"

"Doubtful. It's over a hundred miles from Deming to his place."

"Long way."

"It is. He'll be on the lookout, though. And I wouldn't be surprised if he gets in touch with the *rurales* and put them on high alert. He might even have them search the girls' villages in case we try to take them home."

Coronado nodded. "If they come to my village, we will fight."

"Good. Because I'm thinking we should leave the girls with your people until all this shakes out. In the meantime, we got a good eighty miles to your village, right?"

"More like ninety, *amigo*."

"And every inch of it through Apache country."

"Yes, and with a *bandido* behind every ridge and the *rurales* hunting us every step of the way."

CHAPTER 23

*D*on Antonio Garza was not happy.

One would think, seeing him sitting there beside his bathing pool in the central courtyard of his palatial *hacienda* outside Janos, Chihuahua, Mexico, that he had every reason to be very happy indeed.

This walled courtyard, for example, was incredibly beautiful with its intricate tile mosaics and the classical Moorish arches that led to his principal dwelling, a mansion worth over one million pesos. An armed guard stood atop each wall, turned away, as always, from *Don* Garza and his courtyard activities.

Not that *Don* Garza was in the mood for such activities this morning. In fact, he barely registered the three gorgeous young women attending him this morning, despite the naked perfection of their lithe bodies clearly visible through their sheer outfits.

At 39 years of age, *Don* Garza normally had an insatiable appetite for such women and such activities, but this morning, his mind was possessed by the telegram still clutched in his fist—the telegram and all that it suggested.

Over recent months, someone had killed Sullivan Tucker and Ruble Cochran, striking his business interests in the process.

Now, someone had hit the Silver Spike in Deming, killing two of his men, stealing his girls, and taking another bite out of his empire.

And that wasn't the worst part.

No, the worst part was the same man seemed to be behind all of these attacks. Dos Pesos, Leadville, Santa Fe, and now Deming. Imagining the killer's trail, Garza pictured a 700-mile question mark curling from Leadville through Santa Fe into Dos Pesos and then shooting down its stem to Deming. The only thing needed to complete this punctuation was the dot at the bottom... this place, his *hacienda*, him.

Well, this tall, green-eyed murderer would have a very difficult time reaching *Don* Garza, that was for sure.

As soon as Don Garza received the telegram from *Señora* Flores, he alerted the borderlands *rurales* and told them to be on the lookout for this man, his accomplice, and the missing girls. He also commanded them to notify local *bandidos*.

To the man who apprehended his enemy, Don Garza would give a 50,000-peso reward. But there was one caveat. He wanted the green-eyed man alive. The women, too. The other man, let his bones bleach beneath the sun.

Garza wanted very badly to question the green-eyed man. That interrogation would, of course, take place in the cool damp room beneath his *hacienda*, the same room where he took those who did not follow orders and women who had stayed with him long enough to know secrets but who had also ceased to amuse him. Down in the chamber of *lamentación*, every woman became beautiful and keenly interesting again for a time.

He glanced at the dark-eyed beauty now kneeling beside him, tickling her fingertips up his thigh and showing him the smirk of a mischievous child, and considered taking her down into the chamber just to shake off the bad feeling generated in him by this news about the Silver Spike and the green-eyed man.

But no.

This one—was it Lita?—was young and fresh and willing. Taking her to the chamber would be a waste.

The idea of using the chamber for such a purpose none-theless echoed in his mind. Perhaps another of the girls…

At that moment, however, the door at the opposite end of the courtyard swung open on well-oiled hinges and into view strutted the only other man ever allowed to set eyes, let alone foot, on the inner sanctum of Garza's central courtyard.

The girl at his side stiffened, seeing this man, and pulled the unharmonious halves of her wispy garment together, clutching them over her small, round breasts—an absurd gesture, considering the utter transparency of the sheer gown.

"Do not trouble yourself, my sweet," *Don* Garza told the trembling girl. "*Señor* Rose cares nothing for girls, nothing whatsoever for pleasures of the flesh. He will not even notice your nakedness. *Señor* Rose cares only for killing."

And besides, when it is finally your time to visit the chamber, he thought behind his smile, *it will be my hand, not his, that finishes you.*

"*Don* Garza," Mr. Rose said, showing his bright white smile, "Elena said you wished to see me, *Señor*."

As always, Rose was impeccably dressed, even at this hour, even on short notice. The man's well-tailored suits, perfect posture, neatly groomed hair, and immaculate pencil mustache pleased Garza; not only because they confirmed Rose's consummate professionalism but also because the man's dress and decorum provided delicious irony when considered against the absolute savagery of his profession.

Oliver Rose was the best assassin in the world.

And Garza needed him now.

"Yes, Mr. Rose, I do indeed need you."

Garza read the telegram aloud to the assassin, thereby inadvertently dooming all three women in attendance to eventually visiting the chamber of *lamentación*.

When Garza gave Rose the description of the tall, green-eyed man provided by *Señora* Flores, the assassin smiled.

"It sounds, *Señor*, like our friend is working his way in this direction."

"Exactly," Garza said, pleased that Rose understood so quickly. That was the thing about Rose, the thing that made him so deadly. He wasn't just a killer. Plenty of men would pull a trigger. The man was intelligent. And educated. He had even attended the prestigious West Point Military Academy.

"I still think he's the son of the silent justice I eliminated in Leadville."

"Frank Bullard."

"Yes, *Señor*."

Garza grinned viciously. "I'm still surprised you shot the old man in the back. I thought that went against your code."

Rose spread his hands. "My code is only to do your bidding, *Señor*. Pride does not come into it."

Garza quirked a brow.

Rose allowed a slight grin. "All right. Perhaps pride is part of what I do, but first and foremost, I must kill and survive. Bullard was indeed the first man I ever shot in the back. I didn't have to shoot him in the back. I believe I would have beaten him face-to-face. He was, however, the first man I ever faced who warranted this caution. So you see, *Señor*, in terms of my code, duty comes before pride."

Don Garza twirled one of the trembling girl's tresses

around his finger, tightening it until she muffled a cry of pain. "I don't care one way or the other about your code, *Señor* Rose, so long as you kill this man Bullard."

"If this man is a silent justice, do you really think he will risk an international incident by crossing the border?"

"I am beginning to believe this man will do anything."

"But we have no knowledge of silent justices coming into Mexico before this?"

"None, but we must assume that he is coming."

"Agreed. Have you contacted the *rurales*, *Señor*?"

Garza nodded.

"And the *bandidos*?"

"The *rurales* are to contact them."

"Will they, though, *Señor*? Those *rurales* are just *bandidos* in uniforms. Why would they tell the outlaws and lower their own chances of gaining the reward?"

Garza smiled. "Because they know if they do not do as I say, you will visit them, *Señor* Rose."

"Yes," Rose said, smiling faintly. "Fear is the greatest motivator. Speaking of which, have you reconsidered my suggestion concerning Banderas and McSweeney?"

Garza nodded, doing so now. "I had hoped killing Frank Bullard would put a stop to this, and I did not wish to risk drawing attention, but yes, I suppose it is time to go on the offensive across the border. They have been gathering information?"

Rose nodded. "Frank Bullard had a ranch outside Fredericksburg, Texas. His two sons, Jake and Matt, lived with him there. People say these two are bounty hunters... just like their father."

"A sensible cover story," Garza said. "Do you believe the sons are also silent justices?"

"Either that or they are following unofficially in their father's footsteps."

"So it's them coming for me now?"

"One of them, yes. Jake Bullard, the older brother. The younger brother, Matt, is reportedly recovering from injuries on his ranch."

Garza smiled. "And you know this how?"

"Banderas and McSweeney are as stealthy as they are deadly. They are the only men I trust with such work. Banderas looks like a choir boy, and McSweeney talks like a politician."

"Good. Are you planning to take this Matt Bullard hostage?"

"The thought crossed my mind, *Señor*, but I don't believe that's our best course of action. Texans aren't like other people. They don't understand the concept of surrender. If my men tried taking Matt Bullard alive, he'd cry 'Remember the Alamo' and go down in a blaze of obstinance."

"I believe you are correct. Have them kill him, then. After we take care of Jake Bullard, I don't want to have to deal with his brother."

"My apologies, *Señor*, but eliminating Matt Bullard is not possible at this time. I relocated Banderas and McSweeney. They have been following another lead, and I believe it is time for them to strike."

"Where are they now?" Garza asked, liking the twinkle in the killer's eyes, that bit of comforting barbarism gleaming beneath Rose's outward polish.

"They questioned a man at the telegraph office in Leadville. Apparently, Jake Bullard sent multiple telegrams to a woman. The man they questioned couldn't remember her name, but he remembered the name of the town. Banderas and McSweeney are on their way to a small town called Dos Pesos, New Mexico."

CHAPTER 24

Where they crossed into Mexico, no river or monument delineated the border, but they knew they had crossed all the same. The land was identical to New Mexico and West Texas, long stretches of caliche and cactus between otherworldly buttes and formidable mountain ranges rising jagged and monolithic from the desolation.

And yet they could feel the change, feel Mexico all around them like faint music riding the wind.

But there was something else to the shift, as well; and the farther they traveled, the more strongly they felt this other change, a foreboding that grew more and more terrible until it filled the air like an Aztec death whistle.

Justice could feel the menace all around them, lurking silently just out of sight, watching them from behind ridges and blinds of scrub and from within the dark caves that dotted mesa walls like the empty eye sockets of massive red skulls.

The Apaches were here. And the Apaches knew they were here.

He could feel them watching and waiting.

"I am happy to be back in Mexico," one of the girls, Paulina, said, speaking in Spanish. They had all spoken solely in Spanish since leaving Deming. "But I do not like this place."

"It's better than where we were," one of the quiet girls spoke up, her eyes staring blankly at the dusty oblivion across which they traveled.

They had slept only a few hours, broken camp midmorning, and crossed into Mexico several miles back. Now, the flaming sun was low in the West, and the saguaros' shadows stretched dark and barbed across the hardpan.

Coronado brought his horse close to the wagon. He and Justice had been alternating driving, giving their horses a break.

"There is no water between here and darkness," Coronado said. "Tomorrow morning, about ten miles south, there will be a well."

Justice nodded. "Let's break for camp while there's decent cover. See that cliff yonder?"

Coronado followed his gaze and nodded. "We will be vulnerable from above, but it is still our best option."

"Yeah, we can put our backs to the cliff. The boulders are like walls to either side. We can park the wagon in front. It's the best cover we'll get."

"Do you think they'll come at us tonight?"

He didn't have to mention the Apaches by name and didn't bother hiding the danger from the girls. They all knew the score. The Apache menace thickened the air like the chalky alkali dust swirling in their wake.

"Either tonight or tomorrow at the water, I'd say. One or the other."

Coronado's eyes scaled the cliff they were now approaching. "I still don't like how open we are to attacks from above."

"I'll climb up there and stand watch. You hear gunshots, get the girls on down the road."

They pulled in close to the cliff and made camp between the boulders. They ground hitched their horses, and the girls fed and watered them, using the oats and water barrels they had purchased from the hostler back in Deming.

While Coronado stood watch, Justice began his long ascent with a Winchester slung over one shoulder, a full canteen sloshing on the other, and his pockets stuffed with the jerky and biscuits that would be his dinner.

He wanted to scale the mesa before dark so he could check its top, but also so he could pan his spyglasses across the surrounding country. From up there, he should be able to see for miles.

But despite his urgency, he took his time, not wanting to slip on the crumbling slope and tumble all the way to the hard desert floor.

A few times along the way, he came to ledges of exposed stone. Upon these sturdy perches, he rested and took time to sweep the dimming land with his spyglasses.

Nothing was moving. Nothing broke the pattern. He saw no dust, no flash of glass or metal, nothing.

And yet the feeling of being watched, the sense that their slaughter was a mere nod away, resonated more powerfully than ever.

The question was, resonated from where?

He continued his ascent, grunted his way through the last section, a breathtaking climb up twenty feet of sheer rock face, and topped the mesa just as the sun was melting, red and liquid, like a ball of molten lava, into the far Western horizon.

The men were waiting for him atop the mesa.

The six Apaches stood not ten feet away, staring down at him like so many judges, their faces as stony and stoic as the desert itself. Their rifles were not pointed at Justice, but there could be no beating them. One wrong move on his part and he would fall from the cliff, full of bullet holes.

He stood without touching his weapons and drew to his full height, staring back at them with no expression.

"You have returned to us, Son of Bullard," the oldest of the men said in Apache, and held out his hand, "but we are far from where we last met."

Justice shook the man's hand, careful not to smile or show surprise.

But surprised he was. These men knew him? And knew his father? What were the chances?

Not that slim, he supposed, considering how few men traveled badlands such as these, let alone survived upon them year after year. Also, from what he had learned of his father, Justice thought the man had probably introduced his sons to anyone he respected along the trail. And whether you loved them, hated them, feared them, or fought them, the Apache deserved your deepest respect.

"I am like the wind," Justice said in Apache, the words coming to him easily. "There yesterday, here today."

"And tomorrow?" the man asked. "Where are you taking the women?"

"I return them to their homes," Justice said. He spoke the truth but highlighted a detail he knew would resonate with these warriors. "A Spaniard stole them from their villages. I stole them back. Then I will go to Janos and kill the Spaniard."

The man nodded. "The Spaniards have taken many of our women and children. Our people do not survive long within their walls. Apaches are a free people. We were created as monster killers and make poor slaves. This Spaniard, does he live in the walled *hacienda* between the wooded mountains and Janos?"

Justice nodded. "*Don* Antonio Garza."

"He tortures the women," the man said. "On quiet nights, their screams travel like departing ghosts across the land. We go now to join the Bedonkohe on the Sonora River. We have promised our rifles. Ride with us. Then, when the raiding is over, we will return with you and kill this man Garza. It will be good for the Apache to kill monsters again."

"Thank you for your offer," Justice said, "but I must kill him now."

The man nodded. "So it will be. We cannot go with you all the way to the *hacienda*, but perhaps we can help Son of Bullard for a short time. Come, we have taken an antelope. Join us at our fire, and we will tell you what we know. There is movement upon the land."

CHAPTER 25

Max Jennings was polishing mugs when a pair of strangers strolled into the Third Peso and approached the bar.

Before moving to Dos Pesos, Max had spent most of his life aboard boats—living on them, working on them, captaining them. He'd gone up and down the rivers and sailed the open water, seeing a good portion of the world that way and even staying for a few years on a beach in Ecuador.

He missed life on the water, but now he was too old to do everything you had to do to take care of a boat, and he didn't have the money to hire someone else. During their time in Ecuador, his wife missed New Mexico, so he'd come back with her and built this place, a boat captain stranded in the middle of a waterless desert.

At least, he joked, folks are thirsty here.

And he was thankful for the folks who came into his establishment. Not only because they were paying customers but also because they were what he had in place of life on the water. Their conversation, their stories, their woes and laughter and tales of the beyond... these kept Max going. Once you learned to talk to people—and more importantly, to listen—every day behind the bar was like reading a good book.

And when folks like these two fellas, who he could see at once were from out of town, came walking into the Third Peso, he settled in for an interesting chapter.

"Howdy, gents," Max chimed, walking over to them. "What can I get for you?"

"Whiskey for me, please, good sir," the older of the pair said with an Irish brogue and a kindly smile, "and just a glass of water for my gentle friend here, if you can spare it, sir."

An almost apologetic smile lit the boyish face of the slender man behind the Irishman.

"Coming right up," Max said cheerfully, liking this pair very much. Some folks, the first time you met them, it felt like you'd been friends for years. "But I must apologize, sir. I'm all out of Bushmills." He gave the man a smile and a wink and filled a tumbler with a heavy hand.

"Aye," the man said, "it's a sad state of affairs indeed concerning my beloved Bushmills. Why if a man such as yourself were to stock that amber elixir of the Emerald Isle, cowpokes would line up from here to the Pecos."

"Sadly," Max said, sliding each man's drink toward him, "these folks are sold on rotgut."

"Well, bless their souls," the Irishman said with a rosy-cheeked smile, and lifted his glass, "and here's to your health, sir."

He downed the whiskey with a wincing smile and slid the empty glass forward. "I've had worse. And I thank ye for the heavy pour, my friend. Better hit that again, sir. It's been a long, dusty ride fraught with stage station fare."

Behind him, the boyish fellow sipped gingerly at his

water. As he lifted the glass, his coat spread, and Max was surprised to see a holstered Colt on his hip.

"Where are you boys from, if you don't mind my asking?"

"Well, you've clearly pegged me as a son of dear old Ireland," the talkative man said. "Name's McSweeney, by the way, Angus McSweeney." He stretched a boxy hand across the bar.

Max shook it. "Glad to meet you, Angus. I'm Maxwell Jennings, owner, bartender, and chief bottle washer here at the Third Peso."

"A clever name, that," Angus said, and gestured to the gun-toting man with the boyish face. "This is Valentino Banderas."

Banderas gave another embarrassed smile and stepped forward to shake Max's hand. "Call me Valentine," he said without even a trace of an accent.

"Nice to meet you," Max said. "What line of work are y'all in?"

"We're in cattle, you might say," Angus told him. "Though neither of us knows the first thing about the beasts themselves. No, what we're really in is the business of connecting cattlemen to cattle buyers."

"Good business to be in out here," Max said, "and you've come to the right place if you're looking to meet cattlemen. All the big ranchers come into the Third Peso."

"And no surprise there, given its most excellent steward," Angus said, winking and knocking back his second shot. "But we aren't in town on business, my friend, but rather on a personal matter. We've come all the way from Texas seeking a dear friend of ours. His brother told us he had moved to this area but, alas, he couldn't provide an exact address. It seems our friend had taken up with a lady. Would you happen to know a man named Jake Bullard?"

"Know him?" Max said and slapped the bar. "He comes in

here all the time. A good man, a great man. Only we mostly call him Justice here. Why, he was in here only a couple of weeks ago, just before… oh."

Max frowned, remembering.

"What is it, my friend?" Angus said.

"I'm sorry, fellas. I just remembered. Justice—er, Jake— took off. He left some time ago with another rancher. Headed for Mexico, I think. South, anyway. I'm not sure when he'll be back. Will you be in Dos Pesos long?"

Angus shook his head, frowning. "Sadly, no, my friend, we'll be leaving on the morrow." He reached into his coat, giving Max a glimpse of the Colt he, too, concealed beneath his jacket and plucked a sparkling diamond ring from his pocket. "His brother Matt asked us to bring this ring to Jake. It belonged to their dear old mom, and Jake wants this lady friend to have it. I'm embarrassed to say I can't remember her name."

"Nora," Max said, happy to help these men. Imagine traveling all that way only to find your friend had left for Mexico. "Used to be Nora Eckert. Now's it's Nora Bullard. She and Justice live just south of town on a ranch. Built a new house and barn and everything. Would you like me to tell you how to get there?"

"Oh, my friend," Angus said, sliding the diamond back into his pocket and hiding his pistol again, "there's nothing in the whole wide world that would make this poor old Irishman happier."

CHAPTER 26

"I still can't believe it," Isabela said, an incredulous smile lighting her pretty face. "Do you promise it's the truth?"

She and some of the girls seemed to be coming around a little. They had been through a horrible ordeal. It would take a long time for them to recover—if they ever really managed to recover—but Justice was no stranger to working with folks in the wake of trauma, and he liked what he was seeing from Isabela and some of the other girls. Smiling, laughing, and making conversation were steppingstones from the nightmare they'd suffered back to something far better.

"It's all true," he said.

"I wouldn't believe it if you hadn't brought us the antelope meat," Ana said with a smile almost as incredulous as Isabela's. "*Señor* Coronado said you were quite a man, but this, this is a story I will tell my grandchildren someday."

Justice smiled at that, recognizing another steppingstone, and a major one at that, this girl not only speaking of the future but expecting a good life complete with grandchildren.

Two of the girls remained quiet and withdrawn. Perhaps

they were struggling with all that had happened to them. Or perhaps they were looking ahead and worrying about how people would treat them when they returned home.

Justice didn't know, and there was nothing he could do other than give them space and help them return home safely.

On the advice of the Apaches, they left the main wagon trail when two red mesas rose like twin anvils in the distance.

Bandidos would be waiting for them there, the Apaches said.

They stopped and watered and rested the horses. If the *bandidos* had spotted them, they would still think they were going to continue along the main road.

"Do you really think they're out there, waiting for us?" one of the girls asked with a shudder.

"Count on it," Justice said. Then he turned to another of the girls. "Adelina, are you ready?"

Adelina nodded, looking tough and ready despite the torn, flimsy clothing in which she had escaped. She was the daughter of a teamster, and before her abduction, she had often worked with horses and driven wagons.

"Everyone had better hang on tight," Adelina said. "I will get us there very quickly."

"Good," Justice said, mounting Dagger, "because once they are certain we're leaving the trail, they will come for us in a hurry. We have to reach the ridge before they can intercept us."

By now, the *bandidos* must have spotted them. Good. Because Justice didn't just want to evade them. He wanted to eliminate them.

He did not explain this to the women, however. Some of them were still fragile, of course. For now, he wanted them to focus on just what Adelina had said: holding on tightly until she got them to the place he had described, a dry arroyo just below the highest peak on the ridge a mile to the west.

There was cover there. Not enough cover for two men to fight off the two dozen *bandidos* who would be chasing them, but enough cover for Justice's plan to work.

He took one last swig of water, secured his canteen, and left the trail.

Coronado rode parallel to him, fifty feet to the north, and the wagon followed after them.

Glancing back, Justice saw the girls bouncing and lurching from side to side, but he did not slow.

He knew this would be a close thing, and if he was forced to spring his trap too quickly, they would be battling *bandidos* all the way to Coronado's village.

Looking ahead, he spotted a thick outcropping of cacti and veered northwest. Coronado adjusted his position, and Adelina followed suit immediately.

She's good, Justice thought, grinning grimly. No matter what Garza's people had done to her, she was still a teamster's daughter.

Then he saw dust rise as the *bandidos* raced out of the space between the twin mesas. It was a big cloud, and he suspected the Apaches had been right in their estimations of Fernando Aguilar's forces.

The bandits were moving quickly, pushing their horses.

It was going to be close.

Justice urged Dagger forward, speeding the pace. Coronado adjusted at once.

Looking back, Justice saw the girls reeling in the back of the wagon.

He hoped they held on. Even more, he hoped that Adelina continued to read the terrain expertly.

He and Coronado could scout ahead, avoid obstacles, and forge the best general path, but it was up to Adelina, from second to second, to guide the wagon across this inhospitable terrain.

There was no room for error. A single mistake on her part, and they would be doomed.

And so they raced across this sunbaked land, with the *bandidos* angling toward them and drawing closer every second.

Justice looked ahead and behind, trying to estimate speeds and distances, but such things were difficult to judge across miles, especially on terrain such as this.

But the outlaws were certainly gaining, riding hard but staying in a pack to avoid squandering the advantage of their numbers, thereby exhibiting more discipline than average bands.

The western ridge drew closer, looking like the exposed spine of some great beast buried beneath the land. Justice pointed Dagger toward the center of that imaginary backbone, where the highest peak raised clearly above the rest of the ridge.

The *bandidos* had drawn within half a mile.

It would be a close thing indeed. Soon, they would be in shooting range.

Justice wanted to race forward but couldn't without leaving the girls behind. Meanwhile, he glanced backward and saw a determined Adelina snapping the reins and staring at the ground before her with terrible focus.

The *bandidos* drew within 500 yards.

Then 400 yards.

Then 300.

Up ahead, Justice could now see the wall of mesquite the Apaches had described, as well as the break in that wall that would provide a gateway into the arroyo.

When the *bandidos* drew within 150 yards, Justice wondered again about the unusual discipline they were showing. Why weren't the wilder members of the band firing their rifles?

As Justice neared the arroyo, he looked back and saw the *bandidos* make their move. Half a dozen riders broke away, riding hard toward the wagon.

The main force surged forward, coming for him.

They were only 100 yards out. Why weren't they shooting?

And then, as Justice and Coronado shot into the gap and descended into the arroyo with the girls close behind them and the *bandidos* hurtling to within fifty yards, the shooting began all at once.

For several explosive seconds, hundreds of gunshots cracked the desert air as the Apache band, eighty strong, fired from behind the mesquite, cutting the *bandidos* to the bloodiest of ribbons.

CHAPTER 27

Nora paused at kneading the dough and blew an errant lock from her face.

Beside her, Katie greased the bread pan. The orphan girl was a wonderful addition to the family. Eager and respectful, she helped Nora all day every day.

Katie was particularly good in the kitchen, thanks to her interest, talent, and experience with cooking, and also with Eli, who absolutely adored her.

Since joining their family, Katie had taken the boy under her wing and proved herself to be an excellent teacher. Eli had learned more in the last two weeks, Nora had to confess, than he had in the previous two months.

He adored Katie and wanted to please her.

Nora adored her, too. Katie was truly a daughter to her now.

Nora had enjoyed the extended visit with her own mother and with Faith and Faith's grinning shadow—Justice's charming cousin, Luke—but she was also glad that they had headed back to Texas because it gave her more time with Katie.

One of the things Nora most enjoyed was their conversations. Katie was a smart girl, a reader and a deep thinker, and although she hadn't had the best experience under the nuns at the orphanage, she was nonetheless reverent and deeply interested in the Bible.

"I do have one question," Katie said, helping Nora fill the pans with dough.

"What is it, dear?"

Katie smiled. "I love it when you call me that, Mama."

"And I love it when you call me *Mama*. So, what is your question, dear?"

"I was just thinking about everything you've been through and what Pa is doing now and everything that's happened to me, and well, I guess I don't understand why God lets these things happen."

"You're a smart girl, Katie, and that is a very good question. A question I've asked myself many, many times."

"Why does He?"

"I don't know, dear."

Katie frowned.

"God's ways are not our ways, Katie. It's difficult not to question Him when we are suffering. But oftentimes, when things are going well and you look back, you will see that the best things in your life never would have come to pass if the worst had happened first. When my first husband died, I was heartbroken and frightened. I had no idea how Eli and I would keep the ranch going."

"But if that hadn't happened, you wouldn't have met Justice," Katie said, guessing where Nora was going.

Nora nodded. "That is correct. And if I hadn't met Justice, you would still be enslaved to your uncle in New York City."

Katie shuddered at the thought. "Even that terrible man on the train. If he hadn't done the things he did, I never would have met Justice."

"Exactly," Nora said. "That's why it's so important to focus on our blessings. Only through gratitude and reflection can we understand how God uses the hard parts of our lives to push good things forward."

"Do you think God let my parents die so that I could be here now with you and Eli?"

Nora frowned at that. "God allows suffering, but I'm not trying to say that God brings bad things into our lives to open the door for good things. I'll go back to what I first said. God's ways are not our ways.

"He never leaves us. And if we are faithful and acknowledge Him in all our ways, He will direct our paths. Even during our darkest moments, we are not alone. He is with us. Even when we don't feel Him there, He never forsakes us.

"Usually, it isn't until later—and sometimes, much later—that we understand how He sustained us and used difficult times to build our character and our faith and to put us in certain places and among certain people where we might better serve Him."

Katie nodded. "Thank you for explaining that. The thought troubled me a lot at the orphanage. It made we wonder if God even cared about me."

"God loves you, honey. And He will never forsake you. His love is perfect. Never doubt that. And take strength from it. Even when things look their worst, He is there with us."

"That's comforting, Mama."

"It is. Tell you what, Katie. Tonight, we will memorize the 23rd Psalm. I think you will love it. Now, will you please be a dear and go get three more eggs?"

"Yes Mama," Katie chimed, heading for the door.

"And Katie? Check on Eli while you're out there, okay? Everything's probably fine, but I keep feeling like something is… off. I can't quite explain it, but someday, when you're a mother, you'll know exactly what I mean."

"I think maybe I kind of already do, Mama," Katie said. "I used to watch out for the younger girls at the orphanage, and sometimes, I'd get feelings like that, like maybe something might be wrong. I'll make sure Eli's okay. I'm sure he is." Katie smiled with youthful confidence. "Rafer's with him."

The girl went out the door, and Nora smiled to herself.

How blessed she was. How incredibly blessed. Eli, Justice, Katie, this new house, her neighbors...

And yet, though she wouldn't confess this to Katie, she couldn't help but worry. Receiving the telegram Justice had sent from Socorro had been a wonderful surprise, but why hadn't he sent another from Deming?

Surely he would have reached Deming by now. In fact, unless something had happened, he should already be in Mexico.

So why hadn't he sent another telegram before crossing the border?

Various possibilities crossed her mind, none of them good.

Don't worry, she told herself. Scripture told her not to worry, of course, and beyond that, she had total faith in her husband.

She couldn't help but wonder, however, as she carried the bread to the oven, if something had gone wrong. Is that why she had been feeling such dread all day?

"Mama!" Katie's voice called, full of fear, and Nora's blood turned to ice.

She dropped the bread to the floor, grabbed the shotgun from the counter, and looked out the window.

She saw no sign of Katie.

Instead, she saw a smiling rosy-cheeked man in a business suit, strolling from the barn toward the house.

Nora pulled back both hammers, threw open the door,

and stepped outside, pointing the coach gun at the man who stopped thirty yards away. "Where are my babies?!"

The smiling man swept the hat from his head and gave a bow. "Good afternoon, Mrs. Bullard. Please allow me to introduce myself. My name is—"

"I don't care what your name is. If you don't tell me where my babies are right now, I'm going to fill you with buckshot."

"Oh ma'am, that would be a terrible mistake. If you were to pull those triggers at this distance, you'd make a mess of your sweet girl."

As he said this, a second man, this one slender with a youthful face, stepped from the smokehouse to stand beside the smiling man. The boyish man had one arm around Katie's throat. Seeing the knife in his other hand, Nora slipped her finger from the trigger.

"It's okay, Katie dear," Nora said. "Mama's going to make everything okay."

"Oh my, that's so much better, Mrs. Bullard," the first man said, his voice lilting with an Irish brogue. "I did so hate getting off on the wrong foot with you. An occupational hazard, I suppose."

"What do you want?" Nora said, still pointing the shotgun at the man, though she would never pull the triggers with Katie standing so close—and the smiling man knew that.

But where was Eli? Had they hurt her boy?

"I want *you*, ma'am," the Irishman said. "Now, if you'll kindly lower that shotgun, I'll explain the situation as clearly and concisely as I'm able, hoping you'll forgive me if I occasionally indulge my native-born gift of gab, of course."

Nora lowered the coach gun. Her heart dropped with the double barrels.

Instantly, however, her mind—moving with the supernatural speed of a mother of endangered children—rejected her despair. Hadn't she just told Katie to have faith in God no matter how dire the circumstances?

She straightened her back.

"That's a good lass," the man said. "As I was saying, you'll be coming with us now. Your husband has caused our employer a deal of trouble. Now we must take you to Mexico, so you can talk some sense into Mr. Bullard."

"Garza sent you?"

"Indirectly, yes. Technically speaking, ma'am, it was Mr. Rose who sent us, but yes, it does all boil down to *Don* Garza —and let me suggest, ma'am, that you do address him as *Don*. Otherwise, he'll take you down into his basement and pull out your tongue with a pair of hot metal tongs no matter what your husband does. Come on now, Mrs. Bullard, put down your pop gun and hold out your wrists so my associate can free your dear daughter."

The Irishman reached behind his back and came back around with a pair of handcuffs.

A deep growl sounded, and a multicolored blur flashed around the corner of the barn and leapt into the air.

The man holding Katie turned toward it and screamed— though the sound was sliced in half when Rafer tore the man's throat wide open and knocked him to the ground.

The Irishman gave a cry of surprise, staring at the dog, then turned toward Nora, who had already shouldered the shotgun and sprinted at a sharp angle.

The Irishman dropped the cuffs and raised his hands. He was having trouble holding onto his smile now. "Mrs. Bullard, don't be rash, please. Let's talk about this."

What Nora said next was less for the Irishman—nothing anyone could say to him would matter much longer—and more for her beloved daughter, Katie. "You agents of darkness don't stand a chance. We are on God's side... and He is on ours."

With that, she gave the man both barrels.

Katie rushed to her.

Rafer panted, red mouthed, in that laughing way he had, lifted a leg, and urinated on the man he'd killed.

Eli came tearing around the side of the barn, hatchet in hand, wildfire burning in his eyes, the boy looking every inch the bloodthirsty savage, ready to kill or be killed in defense of his family.

Holding Katie close, Nora smiled at her son, proud of him, loving the fierceness in his eyes and sneering mouth. If he was to become a man on this merciless frontier, he would need that fierceness in spades.

That and, of course, faith in God.

"Come, children," Nora said. "We have learned something. It is time to gather our essentials."

She told herself to leave a note for the hired hands, who were in the back pasture and would come home hungry and confused.

"Where are we going, Mama?" Katie asked.

"I'm not sure yet. Somewhere safe. That's all that matters. We won't be safe here again until your father has killed all of these bad people."

"He will, won't he, Mama?" Eli asked. "Pa will kill them, right?"

"Yes, son," Nora said with a smile. "Your father will kill them all."

CHAPTER 28

I n the aftermath of the slaughter, a couple of the dying *bandidos* who'd survived the initial ambush refused to talk.

Then Justice explained their options. They could tell him what he wanted to know, or he would turn them over to the Apaches and let them extract the answers with their infamous methods.

Then they all talked, and all told the same story.

Don Garza had announced a 50,000-*peso* reward to anyone who could capture Justice alive.

That's why they hadn't shot even after they'd drawn into range. They had planned to kill Coronado, take the girls hostage, and force Justice to come with them.

They had gambled and lost.

But now Justice's situation came into sharper focus. Men all over Chihuahua were looking for a tall, green-eyed man and his accomplices. Coronado was to die. Garza wanted the women, too, if possible, but there was no stated bounty for their return.

Justice was the prize.

He thanked the Apaches for killing his enemies and pledged his undying friendship along with all the spoils of war, including the *bandidos'* horses, weapons, and any possessions in their saddlebags or on their many corpses.

Then, Justice and his friends were on their way again.

Riding close to the wagon, he said, "Adelina, you did an amazing job back there. You saved many lives and did your father proud."

"Thank you, *Señor*," Adelina said, reins in hand. "We should rest the animals soon."

Justice laughed. "Spoken like the true daughter of a teamster, Adelina. We'll rest them soon. But first, let's get back onto the main road. Coronado, there's water between those mesas, right?"

"Yes, my friend. There is a good spring there, along with shade and forage. It is a good place to stop."

"How much farther to your village?"

"Not far. Unless we run into more trouble, we should reach my village tomorrow night."

"That's good to know," Justice said, "though if there is one thing we can definitely expect, it's more trouble."

Coronado grinned. "I've noticed that trouble follows you."

"And I've noticed you follow trouble."

They got back on the road and drove between the mesas, where they discovered the spring and forage Coronado had mentioned. It was a good spot, and Justice wished they could stop for the night, but it was too early, and with so many people hunting him, they had to move quickly.

He surveyed the cloudy sky and decided they had to keep moving once they'd eaten and rested the horses. If he thought the night would be clear, they would hunker down now, doze, and travel by moonlight, but there wasn't even the hint of a breeze. Those clouds weren't going anywhere. The night would be pitch black. They would never be able to follow the road, and going off course in the desert was a sure way to get yourself killed.

So after resting the horses for a spell, they got back on the road again.

Justice was pleased by the girls' attitudes. They had been understandably frightened when the *bandidos* attacked, but they were downright cheerful now, celebrating the deaths of these awful men and every second drawing closer to Coronado's village—and eventually, their own homes.

Justice and Coronado rode ahead, scouting the territory. Massed with cactus and mesquite, the land dipped and rolled. Long views were nonexistent for the moment, so Justice watched the horizon for the dust of approaching riders.

A rabbit darted across their path and disappeared without hesitation into a spiny tangle.

Justice would be glad to finish his business in Mexico and get out of the desert. He missed the forested mountains of home, the river and long grasses, and, of course, his ranch and friends and especially his family.

Then he topped a rise and saw the *rurales* sitting on their horses, barricading the road a few hundred yards ahead.

He reined in, counting the *rurales* automatically.

Bad news. There were twelve of them. Too many to fight. And here, in this place, there could be no outrunning them.

If he had been traveling alone with Dagger, he might be able to escape. Even with Coronado, whose horse was used to the desert, he might have been able to the evade the soldiers.

But in mere minutes, the *rurales* would capture the women. And those poor girls could not return to captivity.

The *rurales* gave a shout and started after him.

Justice wheeled and rode back, his mind racing, and gestured to Coronado.

The fierce Mexican yanked his rifle from its scabbard. "What is it, *amigo?*"

"*Rurales*," Justice said, pulling up to his friend and dismounting.

"What are you doing?" Coronado asked as Justice turned back toward the threat.

"Go back to the girls. The *rurales* want me, not you. I will lead them to the east. They will follow. When they do, continue to your village. And one day, God willing, I will join you there."

Coronado looked at him for a single heartbeat then nodded sharply. "*Vaya con Dios*, my friend."

"*Vaya con Dios*," Justice said and charged hard across the scrub shooting away to the northeast.

The *rurales* shouted and chased after him.

Justice rode hard—but not too hard. With this magnificent horse beneath him, racing across this rolling land, he might very well escape these troopers.

But if he did, they would turn back and find the others in no time.

So he stayed in front of them, leading them farther and farther from the main road but never pushed his stallion, allowing the *rurales* to stay in the race.

He would charge ahead, scan the country, then skyline for a moment, letting them spot him and continue their pursuit.

His mind worked at the possibilities. Could he continue to evade them, then break away hard to the northwest and lose them among the scrubby ridges as darkness fell?

Yes, he thought with a surge of optimism, with this magnificent stallion beneath him, perhaps he could.

But then he topped the rise and the fickle Chihuahuan landscape laughed in the face of his plans, going flat as a coffin lid. And beneath that lid, the desert buried his hopes of losing his pursuers.

Justice turned back, knowing what he had to do but hating the way this maneuver surrendered the gap he had been tending. He raced along the edge of the final slope, hoping he might reestablish and extend his lead and trick them by flying back in the opposite direction. Surely, some of their horses must be tiring by now.

But as he fled, the *rurales*, closer than he'd expected, shouted their warnings.

One of them fired—a big Sharps by the walloping boom of it—and a saguaro near Justice's knee exploded.

He zigged and zagged, but he was out of meaningful cover.

The big Sharps boomed again, and a plume of sand exploded in front of him.

Then he understood.

They weren't firing at him.

They were firing at Dagger.

Given their positions, the lack of real cover, and the range of the Sharps, it was only a matter of seconds before one of those big bullets blew a fist-sized hole through Justice's beloved stallion. And with a round that size, it didn't much matter where the horse was hit. It would spell the end of him.

Justice raised one hand in the air, signaling his intent, and reined Dagger to a stop. Then he dismounted, and raised both hands high above his head, confident his pursuers would not shoot him and squander their big reward.

A moment later, the sneering *rurales* were on him, laughing at their victory and calling him by name as they ordered him to drop to the ground and lock his hands behind his head.

Justice, finally out of options, could only comply. What

troubled him more than capture was the fact they knew his name.

Garza had him now—and Garza knew his name.

CHAPTER 29

Defeat was bitter.

The *rurales'* search was thorough. They stripped him of everything but his clothes.

Opening Justice's money belt, the lieutenant grinned, seeing the fortune inside. Instantly, he lifted his blue uniform shirt and fastened the belt around his own waist.

Then he came over and patted Justice on the shoulder, laughing. "*Señor, muy encantado de conocerte.*"

Justice wanted to throttle the grinning lieutenant, but with his wrists tied and the *rurales* surrounding him that wasn't possible at the moment. "First impressions can be deceiving," he responded in Spanish. "Later, we will see how pleased you are to meet me."

The lieutenant's smile held—barely—but his eyes darkened. "I am pleased to hear you speak Spanish, *Señor*. It will make my job easier. But certainly, *Señor*, in your position, you are not threatening me?"

"I don't make threats," Justice said. "I only tell folks how things are going to go."

The lieutenant chuckled. "Please tell me, *Señor*. How are things going to go?"

"That all depends on if you have the sense to do what you should do."

"Oh? And what should I do?"

"Well, if you let me go now, you can keep my money, and I will give you an additional 60,000 pesos."

The lieutenant threw back his head and laughed. In a small room like a jail cell, the sound of his laughter would have echoed loudly, but out here in the open desert, it faded quickly.

"Oh *Señor*," the lieutenant said, wiping tears from the corners of his eyes, "I, Lieutenant Santiago Ruelas, am very pleased to meet you indeed. You speak Spanish and you make jokes. Where are these 60,000 *pesos* of which you speak? Not in your pockets, not in your saddle bags. You have it buried, perhaps, here in the desert?"

The other *rurales* laughed at their commander's joke.

"You let me go, I'll wire it to you."

"Wire it to me?"

"Yes. You have my word."

Ruelas shook his head. "Your word? I think I prefer your money to your word." He slapped his shirt where the money belt now rode then patted Justice's holstered Colts, which he'd also fastened around himself. "And your weapons and especially this fine stallion you have given me. Not to mention the 50,000 *pesos* promised by *Don* Garza."

"I will give you more."

The lieutenant's smile died. "This money you offer, it is like a ghost. Much as I would be if I were to fall for your trick. I would not face *Señor* Rose for all the *pesos* in the world, you see, for I am not a fool."

"You're a fool if you don't accept my offer."

The smile returned, but there was no humor in it this time. "Why is that, *Señor?*"

"Because it's your only chance to save yourself. If you don't release me now, you'll be dead before you see a single *peso* of Garza's money."

Ruelas shook his head, mock woefully. "It is a sad thing to see a powerless man make such humiliating threats."

"I told you. I don't make threats. I just tell folks how things are going to go."

Ruelas slapped Justice hard across the face.

Justice didn't try to block it, but he did turn with the blow, taking some of the force of it. Nonetheless, his face burned, and he tasted blood.

"No, *Señor,*" Ruelas said, eyes blazing now. "It is I who says how things will go. You foolish *Norteamericanos* come down here, thinking you are special? You are not special, *Señor.* You are a dead man."

Ruelas spat on the ground between them as if sealing a covenant. "You would already be food for the buzzards if not for the reward. But we are taking you back to the garrison, where I will send a telegram to *Don* Garza, and tomorrow, *Señor* Rose will come for you. He would likely shoot you in your cell, but I believe *Don* Garza wishes to question you. And that, *Señor,* is bad news for you, because *Don* Garza has a special room in his *hacienda,* a room where he makes people his playthings, a room with many machines and tools, where he does things that make the torture of Apaches look like a doting mother's love."

Ruelas stared into Justice's eyes and poked him in the chest. "*That* is what is going to happen, *Señor.*"

Ruelas climbed into Justice's saddle atop Dagger, who snorted and made short, choppy steps back and forth until Justice calmed the stallion with his voice.

Justice had taken measure of this lieutenant and knew

Ruelas was the sort of man who would beat Dagger if the stallion gave him trouble.

If that happened, Justice would fight them. And if he fought them, they would hurt him badly. They wouldn't kill him, of course, because that would forfeit the bounty. But they would throw him down and put the boot leather to him, and he needed his health now.

Escaping would be much harder with broken bones.

So Justice calmed Dagger and did not resist the *rurales* when they loaded him onto the lieutenant's horse.

They rode southeast for hours, passing out of the desert scrub and into a new region. The land rose beneath them, and the mesas and stark plains gave way to rugged mountains with stony peaks jutting up from their forested bulks. They stopped between the mountains and let the horses drink at trickling streams.

They passed through a few villages. The afternoon melted into evening. Justice rode in silence at the center of the single-file column, listening to the men, and knew that they were racing against darkness to reach the garrison, which waited on the other side of the tall mountain they were now scaling.

Ruelas sent a man ahead to send a telegram to Garza.

So they must be getting close, Justice reckoned. He had a good feel for territory, and his sense of direction never failed him. He judged that they had been moving steadily southeast and drawing closer to both Janos and Coronado's village.

Consulting the map he had committed to memory, he believed they were presently on the same latitude as Coronado's village, perhaps fifteen or twenty miles to the east across a belt of forested mountains and shallow lakes.

The horses plodded up the steep slope carrying them up the final mountain. To their right, the mountain fell away into a forested gorge. Beyond that, mountains stretched away where the sun was setting in the west, its dying light red upon a distant lake.

Up and up they traveled.

Somewhere on the opposite side of this incline, the road would descend to the garrison, where more soldiers would be waiting and where these men would lock Justice in a cell from which there could be no escape.

Justice remained calm and waited, and then, finally, as the light of day dimmed further and the trail skirted a cliff that fell away down a long slope of loose scree toward a forested gorge, Justice made his move.

CHAPTER 30

Slipping his feet from the stirrups, Justice leaned toward the cliff and threw himself from the horse, pushing away with his legs so that his fall carried him off the trail. He twisted, hit the mountainside with his shoulder, and tumbled down the slope of rocks and loose dirt, grunting as he banged into larger stones and snapped through small saplings that jutted from the hillside.

These obstacles somewhat slowed his bouncing, sliding descent, and that was good, because he was gaining speed as he tumbled, wrists tied, down the mountainside.

Justice kept his chin tucked and tried to protect his face with his bound wrists, but rolled and bounced, taking a beating, and occasionally slammed painfully to a near standstill before sliding down the next rough slope, which tore at his clothing and sandpapered the skin from his exposed flesh. A gunshot sounded above, followed by a rapid-fire volley, but if any of the bullets passed close to him, he couldn't know.

Then the ground disappeared beneath him, and he was falling through open air, tumbling through the gathering darkness, gritting his teeth and trying to get his boots beneath him before impact.

He tucked his chin again and pulled his elbows tight and raised his fists in front of his face as if preparing to take a haymaker. Then his feet slammed home and the rest of him pounded after them, hammering him, praise God, not into a makeshift grave of gravel and pine needles but ten feet of cold, spring-fed, lake water.

His boots pounded into the floor of the lake, and he jarred to a stop. Impact knocked the air from his lungs, and it was all he could do to keep from gasping reflexively and filling his lungs with water.

Instead, he pushed off with his feet and kicked toward the surface, making short strokes with his bound wrists in an awkward doggy paddle that carried him up and up until he broke the surface and inhaled desperately, filling his lungs with cool, delicious air.

Everything hurt, but he exploded with the most primal joy of all. He was free and, against all odds, alive. The thrill of this fact filled him with strength and fresh resolve. He pushed through his pain, treading water and getting his breathing under control, and set his mind to the task of reading this new situation.

Far up the slope, men were shouting. There was no more shooting, of course. Lieutenant Ruelas wouldn't risk losing 50,000 *pesos* so brazenly, not in his own backyard with many men at his disposal, knowing that Justice was a stranger here, a man likely very badly injured from his fall and with no bearings or friends to help him.

But for as much as Justice's body hurt, those assumptions would be wrong. Because despite his many bumps and abrasions, the pitiful state of his clothing, and the fact that he had wrenched his left shoulder, split one eyebrow open, and likely cracked a rib or two, he sensed no injuries serious enough to slow, let alone stop him now.

Also, the map was a living thing in Justice's mind, and he was nowhere near as lost as his adversary likely assumed. He just needed to make his way steadily westward across these mountains and there he would find Coronado's village and friends the *rurales* would not be counting on.

Up above, men continued to shout, making a lot of noise as they tied off ropes and sent soldiers down the slope after him.

Having regained his breath, Justice returned to his awkward doggy paddle and crossed the narrow lake to its western shore, where he slipped into the stubby pines and started up the gentler slope, using the trees to propel himself uphill and away from his enemies.

It was dark in the woods of the western slope, but his eyes adjusted to the gloom, and he made good time, moving away from his pursuers, especially when he read the fold of the land and turned, following a downward sloping bank that carried him around the base of the huge mountain.

Reaching mostly level ground, he ran with long strides, ignoring his pain, which did not matter now, and minding his breathing, which mattered very much.

Justice was long and strong and tough, with incredible endurance and not an ounce of quit in him. Moreover, he was powered by the ultimate motivation: survival.

So with every passing minute, he moved farther away from these lesser men who fumbled through the wilderness after him, wondering which way he had gone, pushing themselves not as a matter of survival but in hopes of perhaps gaining some small share of their commander's prize.

It was no contest.

Later, when darkness was complete, Justice paused and caught his breath and stilled his heart and mind, listening. He heard nothing from his pursuers but a faint holler far behind him and knew that he had managed to pull away by a solid mile, perhaps even two or three. Now, his pursuers would panic, worrying they might lose him.

He walked rapidly through the darkness, pausing only to slake his thirst at a trickling spring, then walked again until he discovered an outcropping of basaltic stone. Against this rough surface, he raked his wrists back and forth, fraying the ropes until they sprang away, freeing his hands.

He grinned in the darkness, flexing his big hands.

Now, he thought darkly, now, they quit worrying about losing me and start worrying about me finding them.

CHAPTER 31

Clouds shifted overhead, parting momentarily, and a shaft of moonlight briefly illuminated the fold between the mountains.

Crouching beside a stream that tumbled down the pass he'd been scaling, Justice scooped mud and slicked it over his exposed skin. The contact stung his many abrasions, but he slathered the cool mud over his arms and neck and face. Then he streaked his already filthy clothes with dark mud, camouflaging himself against the night forest.

The temperature had dropped sharply, and Justice shivered involuntarily.

He was cold and hungry, hurting and tired, but he did not allow his mind to cling to these things. Nor did he allow prolonged conjecture, hopes and worries, or thoughts of home to weaken him.

Until he escaped these mountains, he must be more beast than man. Beasts did not worry, did not feel self-pity, did not cloud their minds with hypothetical possibilities. Likewise, Justice trusted his instincts and focused on his senses, especially his sense of hearing, which sharpened in the cold, thin air of the mountains.

Satisfied with his impromptu camouflage, he moved away from the stream, leaving clear boot prints for a good distance in the mud, then backtracked carefully, hopped onto a stone to one side of the tracks he'd left, and slipped behind a cluster of pines, where he picked up a large, jagged stone and leaned against a boulder, resting his body while he listened and watched, waiting with the terrible patience of a wild predator.

Time passed. Ten minutes, twenty, thirty.

His body recovered. The pain remained, of course, and he continued to ignore it. But his muscles appreciated the rest he was giving them along with the water he'd drunk. He needed food, too, but over his half-remembered lifetime, he had conditioned his body to go long stretches without nourishment, so this did not trouble him.

Nearly an hour later, when he heard the whispers of approaching men, Justice rose from his seat, and stood behind the trees, clutching the rock, his body thrummed with deadly force.

The two soldiers came up the slope, huffing and puffing, and making a lot of noise clattering over stones and breaking branches.

One soldier seemed to be having a hard time. Lagging twenty feet behind the other man, he dug the butt of his carbine into the ground and pushed off, using the rifle like a walking stick as he struggled uphill. Even in the dim light, Justice could see a long, bloody scratch on the man's grimacing face.

The soldier in front was squinting at the ground thirty feet from Justice's position. Any moment now, he would spot the tracks.

"Let's take a break," the man in back complained. "I will give you a cigarette."

"I don't want a cigarette," the other man grumbled. "I want to catch this *gringo*."

"He is probably miles away."

"No. We have seen too many signs. What other way would he go? He's hurt, Emilio. He fell all the way down the mountain. And no injured thing runs uphill."

"Then why are we climbing this hill?" Emilio whined.

"He has to be climbing this hill. Where else is there to go? But I'm telling you. He stuck to the low ground while he could. The lieutenant is right. He will come out between the mountains. Either just down the other side of this one, where the water runs, or farther to the west, where Pedro shot that big bull elk."

"Come then, let us sleep. The lieutenant and the others will wait for him in those places."

The first man shook his head. "When Rose arrives tomorrow, do you want to be the one who let this *gringo* get away?"

That spurred Emilio. He braced the butt of the carbine on the ground, grunted, and pulled himself up. "I wish I had never joined the *rurales*."

"Look," the man in front whispered, coming to the tracks. "I told you he came this way."

The man lifted his head, scanning the darkness, and moved forward, following the tracks.

He passed within two feet of Justice, who waited patiently.

Emilio hurried after his friend. He no longer used the carbine as a crutch. Holding the rifle across his body, he grinned and hobbled after his friend. "Wait for me."

He reached Justice's hiding spot just as the other man reached the end of the tracks twenty feet uphill.

When Emilio passed the trees, Justice slipped silently

behind him and brought the rock down violently with both hands. Its jagged edge smashed into the back of Emilio's skull, crushing it, and the *rurale* fell heavily to the ground.

Justice scooped up the carbine. Another man would have needed time to examine the gun, but Justice had an affinity for weapons and far more experience than he consciously remembered, and his hands did the work as he raised the stubby rifle.

Besides, luck was with him tonight. Emilio had been carrying a Winchester 1873, a weapon Justice had fired thousands of times.

Twenty feet away, the other *rurale* wheeled at the sound of his friend hitting the ground. He gave a startled cry and shouldered his weapon.

He and Justice fired at the same moment.

CHAPTER 32

The man's bullet burned across Justice's left arm just below the shoulder.

Justice's bullet hit the man in the center of the chest and put him down.

Moving quickly, Justice rushed uphill, ready to shoot again if the man reached for his carbine, which had fallen a few feet from his twitching body.

But when he reached the man, the *rurale* was already sliding into death.

Justice crouched, retrieved the man's rifle, slung it over his shoulder, and then searched the corpse before heading back down hill to search Emilio.

Between the two men, he came away with heavy coils of rope, a few *pesos*, a stick of jerky, a decent hunting knife, and two bandoliers of extra ammunition.

Now, it was time to move. Because if there were other hunters on the mountain, they would come running toward the gunshots.

He sprinted uphill, considering what he'd learned from the men.

Rose was coming in the morning.

Meanwhile, Lieutenant Ruelas expected Justice to flee the mountains downhill from this point or a short distance farther to the west.

Which meant he should stay in the mountains and travel north and west to avoid getting funneled into a kill zone.

And yet…

The lieutenant had taken Dagger, not to mention Justice's other possessions. And there was the matter of the promises Justice had made and the lieutenant had mocked.

How many men would be waiting at each location? How many were behind him now, hunting his tracks? How many had Ruelas sent back to the garrison? How many others had come here from there?

Where was the lieutenant himself? Had he returned to the garrison, leaving his men to capture Justice?

No. Because Rose was coming in the morning.

Ruelas was out here somewhere, desperate to capture Justice before Rose arrived. He would take the best watch, the place he believed Justice would attempt to flee the mountains.

Based on what these men had said, then, the lieutenant would be just down the opposite slope, where the base of this mountain met that of the next.

Justice changed directions sharply and crossed the stream. Moving as quickly and quietly as he could, he headed south, crested the mountain, and stared down the other side, avoiding the slope that descended more gently into the kill zone and instead following a route that would drop him a good distance to the east of the lieutenant's likely position.

The question was, why didn't they expect him to go this way? What lay ahead on this side that would keep him from—

And then, suddenly, he was teetering at the edge of a

sheer cliff, staring out across the void, above which clouds churned, casting the land beyond in a patchwork quilt of shadow and moonlight.

The cliff ran the length of the mountain's southern edge, dropping at this point roughly a hundred feet to the rocks below, behind which the forest rode a gentler slope down to where the land flattened out in the valley.

Stepping back from the cliff, Justice took the opportunity to eat the jerky and examine the carbines. Both weapons were serviceable and fully loaded, save for the single round the one man fired at him and which he now replaced.

Content with his weapons, Justice examined the rope as best he could in the darkness, checking for any weaknesses and estimating its length. He found no problems and believed each rope was one hundred and fifty feet in length.

He tied the ropes together, checked and double-checked the union, then wrapped the three-hundred-foot rope around the trunk of a sturdy tree ten feet back from the edge with half the rope coming around each side.

These ends he tossed over the cliff. Then he slung the carbines over his shoulders crossways and stood between the two ropes with his back to the cliff.

He picked up the ropes and wrapped them around his waist, crossing them along his lower back. He stepped over the ropes, took them between his legs, and brought both ropes around to his right side.

He tested the rig, holding on with his left hand to the rope that ran from him to the tree, and leaned back. There was no give at all until he played out some slack with his right hand.

Satisfied, he got into position at the edge of the cliff with his back to the void. Placing his heels at the edge, he leaned back, trusting the ropes. Then he took that first step and let a little rope feed through his right hand.

Careful to lean back into it, he moved slowly but steadily, rappelling down through the darkness. His injured ribs screamed about it, but he paid them no heed, and a short time later, he touched down on the rocky talus at the base of the cliff.

He showed the night a fierce grin, unslung a carbine, and moved off through the woods to the southwest, meaning to come out behind the lieutenant and his waiting men.

CHAPTER 33

The Norteamericano *will come this way,* Lieutenant Santiago Ruelas assured himself for the hundredth time. *He will come limping off the mountain and follow the creek, looking for a farm where he might steal a horse or find a rifle or perhaps a place to hide. But instead of these things, he will find me, waiting here with my men behind these boulders.*

Again, he imagined these things happening, pictured the *gringo* injured and exhausted, limping alongside the creek and passing these boulders five feet from where Ruelas and his men would be waiting on both sides of the stream.

He pictured the *Norteamericano* falling to his knees with a cry of anguish, too weak and spirit broken to even resist as they closed on him, this time securing his hands behind his back with actual handcuffs and forcing him to stumble behind the horses with a rope secured around his waist.

Ruelas tried to smile, picturing the fortune *Don* Garza was offering as a reward, but no matter how many times Ruelas replayed this scene in his mind, he could not make it wholly real, could not quite believe it.

So many things might have gone wrong. Surely, the

Norteamericano was badly hurt after falling down the mountain. Perhaps he had succumbed to injuries and they would never find him.

Or perhaps he was not so badly injured, but he would not follow the stream and would scale the next mountain, heading west instead of coming here. That would not be so bad as long as he tried to exit the next gap, where Guillermo and his men were waiting, or traveled farther on to the river, where Eduardo would capture him.

But what if he confounded all their expectations and headed steadily north, away from their traps?

What if he staggered off a cliff and broke his neck where they would never find him?

What if the gunshots they had heard were Emilio and Matteo killing the *Norteamericano?*

Ruelas badly wanted the 50,000-*peso* reward. After having the *gringo* in his possession, how couldn't he? But the longer the night went on and the more these possibilities plagued his mind, the less he cared about the money, and the more he worried about the coming day, when *Señor* Rose would arrive from the *hacienda*, expecting to find Jake Bullard behind bars.

I was a fool to send Gonzalo ahead, Lieutenant Ruelas told himself.

He knew that now, but how could he have guessed the crazy *Norteamericano* would throw himself from his saddle and down that long cliff?

They were so close to reaching the garrison. He just wanted to send *Don* Garza the good news.

And Gonzalo had. Woefully, he had raced back to the garrison and sent the telegram as Lieutenant Ruelas had directed.

Yes, as time crept closer to Rose's arrival, Ruelas found it even harder to imagine earning the reward and even easier to imagine being gunned down as an example to the other *rurales.*

Picturing Rose's face, he broke out in a cold sweat.

Be patient, he told himself. *Be smart. This is a hunt. And the best times for hunting are dusk and dawn. In mere minutes the sun will rise and then the* Norteamericano *will come stumbling out of the forest and into your grasp.*

Easy to say, hard to believe. That was the trouble.

He glanced over his shoulder to where he had picketed the *gringo's* fine stallion. Never before had Ruelas seen such an amazing horse. Even in the dim light, its magnificence gleamed.

An almost irresistible urge seized Ruelas, telling him to cut his losses, mount the stallion, and run for his life.

But he was no coward. He did not wish to die in this blue uniform, but he nonetheless wore it with pride.

He would not run now. What use would a fine stallion be to a man who loathed himself as a deserter?

He would stay.

This thought brought him strength. He would stay, capture the *Norteamericano,* and bring himself not only money but honor. Later, as a captain of the *Guardia Rural,* he would look back to this time as the moment that tested his resolve and changed his life forever.

With the darkness fading around him, he whispered to his soldiers, "Ready now. Any second, the sun will rise, and the *gringo* will come to us."

Both men hunkered down to await the sun.

The sky grew lighter.

Ruelas risked a glance beyond the boulders and saw everything in greater detail: the creek, the rocks, the trees, the slopes rising in opposite directions.

The *Norteamericano* would reveal himself soon. Any second now. Reulas grinned, feeling it in his bones.

Then, as the sun finally peeked over the eastern horizon, a deep voice behind them said, "Put down your weapons and get your hands in the air."

Ruelas yelped with surprise and started to turn.

Beside him, Bernal raised his weapon.

A rifle barked, incredibly loud and close, and Bernal fell to the ground, dead as a stone.

Ruelas and Leonel dropped their weapons and raised their hands as the *Norteamericano* emerged from behind the horses.

"*Señor*," Ruelas said, trying to make sense of what was happening, "how did you…"

"You boys keep your hands in the air. I'd rather not kill you, but I will if you so much as sneeze."

The *Norteamericano* dealt with them one at a time, relieving them of their weapons and money, then used their own handcuffs to chain them together around a nearby tree.

"I showed you mercy," the man named Bullard said, mounting his stallion and driving off the other two horses. "If you ever come after me again, I won't show you a shred of mercy. *Comprendeme?*"

Ruelas nodded.

Yes, he understood.

As the *Norteamericano* rode into the west, Ruelas definitely understood that the man had shown him mercy… which was something he knew better than to expect from *Señor* ROSE, who might already be on his way to the garrison.

CHAPTER 34

Picturing the map in his mind, Justice rode Dagger westward along the southern edge of the mountains, staying a few hundred yards to the south. He rode at a comfortable pace, wanting to preserve Dagger because he knew other *rurales* could spot him any minute.

One mountain folded into another. Justice stuck to the south side of a low ridge crowned in scrub and passed the mountain gap without incident.

With Ruelas miles behind him, he stopped to check his packs. Everything was there.

He ate some jerky and an airtight of peaches, wishing he had time to brew some Arbuckles. Instead, he settled for a good slug of water, then offered Dagger some water and the last apple from his saddle bag.

He talked softly to his stallion, who nuzzled him, snuffling, showing Justice he was happy to be reunited.

Justice checked the pigging strips he'd used to tie the *rurales'* weapons to his saddle. They'd hold. Then he checked his own rifle and shotgun and the pistols he'd recaptured from Ruelas. Everything was fully loaded.

As he got underway again, he focused his mind.

Everything had changed.

Garza and Rose knew he was in Chihuahua now. They also knew who he was. Which led to a troubling thought. Was his family in danger?

There was nothing he could do about that now, and he had faith in his wife. She was a lot tougher than her pretty face would've led anyone to believe.

Did Garza and Rose know Justice had escaped from the *rurales*?

If so, would they flee?

No. Rose would not. But perhaps Garza would. That was if he knew Justice had escaped.

Had Lieutenant Ruelas informed Garza of the escape? Or had he held his tongue, hoping to fix the problem before Garza learned of the escape?

There was no way of knowing.

Justice realized now that he should have interrogated the lieutenant, but at the time he had been understandably eager to leave the scene. The gunshots were likely to summon others, after all.

Whatever the case, he had to adjust to this new scenario. He had to move on Garza's *hacienda* as quickly as possible.

Or rather, as quickly as *intelligently* possible.

If the *rurales* had never spotted him, he might have been able to slip into Garza's compound and surprise the man. But that was no longer possible.

Now more than ever he needed the help of Coronado.

He thought back to what the girl had told him of the *hacienda*. A garrison-style wall surrounded the million-*peso* mansion with a tower in each corner.

In two of these towers, she had said, men stood behind large guns with many barrels.

Which meant Garza probably had at least a couple of Gatling guns up there.

Isabela had ridden with her father to Garza's *hacienda* during the seasonal visit. The people of her village made colorful clothing, blankets, and pottery and trusted her father to sell these for the best prices to people like Garza and other wealthy men in the region.

They hadn't known then, of course, that Garza was a monster.

Sadly, her people still didn't know. Or at least they hadn't until Coronado, Isabela, and the others reached home.

He had to find Coronado's village, get his friend, and get to the *hacienda* before Garza could run. Because if they let Garza get away, there was no telling when they would manage to track him down again.

With a man as wealthy and cautious as Garza, they might never get that chance.

These were Justice's thoughts as he skirted another mountain and came to a shallow river. He rode along the shore for a moment, studying the riverbed and looking for dangers, when a shot rang out from the northeast.

Glancing in that direction, he saw four *rurales* around three hundred yards out, riding full speed toward him.

"Come on," he said, and urged Dagger into the water.

They crossed the river with no problem.

Another shot rang out.

Justice plunged through the riverside brush, burst out the other side, and leaned across the stallion, letting Dagger give it all he had.

When he had stretched their lead to five hundred yards, he eased up, letting Dagger relax a bit.

If he had more time, he would ride south to throw off the soldiers, but there wasn't time. He had to find Coronado and go get Garza before the snake slithered away.

He studied the land ahead, running his eyes forward across the topography like a fingertip tracing a map. Every now and then, he looked back and judged the distance. Whenever his pursuers started gaining on him, he galloped away from them, reestablishing his lead.

No way those boys could hit him at four or five hundred yards while galloping. No way.

The question was, what should he do about them?

He had hoped, seeing Dagger's speed, they would have quit the chase. But these boys were dedicated. Not a one of them had fallen away.

Coronado's lake was only a short distance ahead. Perhaps two or three miles. Ringed in mountains, it would be a good place to set up an ambush. But he would need a better lead for that to work.

So he pushed Dagger harder, pulling away from the *rurales*, who seemed to be dropping back a little on their own. Geldings issued by the Mexican government were no match for a prize stallion like Dagger.

By the time he reached the lake, the soldiers were no longer visible behind him. He knew they would keep coming, following his tracks, which he hadn't bothered to disguise.

On the far side of the shallow lake, he saw tendrils of smoke rising from the tiny village.

Which would have been a wonderful sight to behold if another sight hadn't eclipsed it so wholly.

Because straight ahead, not even 100 yards away, several horsemen armed with rifles were riding straight at him.

CHAPTER 35

Coronado grinned. "You escaped."

Justice pulled up to him. "Actually, I'm in the process of escaping."

"They coming for you now, *amigo?*"

"Oh yeah."

"How many?"

"Four."

"How far back?"

"Quarter mile, maybe. Probably closer now."

Coronado spoke with authority to the other men, and they quickly left the road and dismounted behind cover, spreading out on both sides of the trail.

Justice joined them.

A moment later, the first of the *rurales* rode into view, hunched low, eyes wary, his horse huffing and foaming at the mouth.

No one fired a shot, letting him come on until another rider appeared and then another. The fourth rode into view just as the first drew even with Justice and the villagers, who opened up all at once.

It was a massacre. The *rurales* didn't even have a chance to return fire. Miraculously, none of their horses were even grazed.

Justice explained the situation.

"I am glad you still live, my friend," Coronado said. "We were just on our way to break you out."

Justice shook his head. "I told you to wait."

Coronado shrugged. "I've never liked taking orders much."

Coronado briefly introduced the other men. They were all from his village and ranged in age from late teens to early fifties.

One of the older men shook Justice's hand, his fierce eyes gleaming with half-shed tears. "Thank you, *Señor* Bullard, for bringing my daughter Isabela home again."

"Glad we got her back to you, sir," Justice said. Then, turning to Coronado, he said, "We have four more horses and seven more 1873 carbines, counting the ones lashed to my saddle. You have more men willing to fight?"

Coronado smiled darkly. "Of course. My people might fish and farm, but we are warriors at heart. Most prefer a bow, but for this, they will carry a rifle."

"Sounds good. Let's go get them. We don't have a minute to waste."

When they rode into the village, scruddy-looking dogs barked, and folks rushed out to meet the riders. The girls they had rescued saw Justice and cheered, and everyone crowded around.

Coronado's voice boomed, bringing them to order. He explained the situation and asked for volunteers and a dozen men stepped boldly forward, most holding a bow.

While Justice appreciated their enthusiasm, they couldn't just go riding in there, not with a pair of Gatling guns waiting for them.

They needed a plan, and he reckoned he had cooked one up while evading the *rurales*. "*Señor*," Justice said, turning to Isabela's father. "How would you like to get revenge on Don Garza?"

CHAPTER 36

The soldier standing guard snapped to attention, saluted, and opened the gate, letting the black carriage enter the garrison of the *Guardia Rural*.

The driver pulled up to the main building, stopped the horses, hitched them to the post, and hurried around to open the door for his single passenger, who flowed as smoothly as a patch of midnight from the compartment and paused to study the adobe building with just a hint of amusement lifting the corners of his neatly trimmed mustache.

The almost smiling man was Oliver Rosedale, known in this country and the Western United States as Rose—whether that be *Señor* or *Mister* Rose varied, but no one dared to so much as guess at a first name.

He had abandoned his first name and extended last name in the East, along with a young wife, his budding military career, and the family fortune he had never really wanted.

Like most who ventured into the West, Rose was determined to make a name and a new fortune for himself. He had already achieved both of those goals.

But unlike most folks who went west, Rose was a cold-blooded killer who actually enjoyed the work. He lived to kill, in fact. And while he demanded comfort and respect, he really cared only for besting other men in contests to the death.

Beyond his penchant for killing, Rose was a supremely controlled individual. His dress, carriage, and speech were impeccable. He did not drink or steal or run with sporting women and he only enjoyed gambling when the games involved skill and analysis. Poker amused him, blending these things with luck; but he had no interest in games of chance like roulette. One might as well bet his fate on the flip of a coin.

Everything to him was control and deportment, skill and the use of skill under pressure, matching his effectiveness against the effectiveness of other men. The more primal the stakes, the better. Competing for anything less than life and death was simple diversion.

Rose's half-smile held as the door to the garrison building swung open.

The sergeant on duty went ramrod straight and saluted, not meeting Rose's eyes as he said, "Good morning, *Señor* Rose. Please come inside, *Señor*."

If only Rose's West Point instructors could see him now. He might not hold an official rank, but he certainly held sway over these soldiers, who showed him more respect than they would a decorated general.

"Where is he, sergeant?" Rose asked, scanning the cells and seeing only a peasant with blackened eyes.

"*Señor*," the man said, "Lieutenant Ruelas regrets to inform you that the prisoner escaped... prior to reaching the garrison, *Señor*."

"Escaped?"

"Yes, *Señor*. Prior to reaching the garrison, *Señor*."

"You already said that."

"Yes, *Señor*. I apologize, *Señor*. I just didn't want you to think—"

"You didn't want me to think it was your fault."

"That is correct, *Señor*. I did not want you to think I let the prisoner escape. I never even saw him, *Señor*." The sergeant's eyes flicked hopefully to Rose and leapt away like fingers from red-hot iron.

"You have no reason to fear, sergeant," Rose said with a smile. "Now, tell me. Where is the lieutenant?"

As the sergeant explained the situation, Rose did not allow his irritation to show.

The carriage could not travel to where Ruelas was positioned. That meant Rose would have to ride a horse.

Rose hated riding horses. It was uncomfortable, and he invariably got his clothes dirty. Worse still, he would almost certainly ruin his shoes.

Additionally, of course, he had been looking forward to killing this silent justice, Jake Bullard, the son of Frank Bullard, whom he had already killed.

Rose had never quite quieted his mind after shooting the old man in the back. The opportunity had presented itself, and he had taken it, knowing Frank Bullard was a real threat.

He had not anticipated, however, the self-loathing he had felt ever since. The fact that he'd shot the man without warning from behind throbbed in Rose's consciousness like a sliver of bone jammed between two molars.

This self-loathing had nothing to do with morals, of course. Rose was not weighed down by anything ridiculous like that. Nor, contrary to what *Don* Garza apparently believed, did Rose ascribe to any code—no more than any man's pattern of actions and reactions could be called a code.

What bothered Rose was that he had evaded his greatest challenge. Bullard was by all accounts a worthy opponent.

Beating him would have meant something. So why had he shot him in the back?

He wasn't entirely certain.

And that lack of certainty bothered him more than anything else. Always before, he had relished any challenge. So why had he shot Bullard in the back?

He'd seen the man and taken the shot. That was all. He had killed Bullard before the silent justice had even understood he was in danger.

Why?

Certainly, he hadn't felt anything like fear. Rose feared no man.

But there had been something, some voice not entirely his own whispering deep inside him during that moment, encouraging him to take the shot… just in case.

A thing like doubt.

Up until that moment, Rose had never even considered that he might be vulnerable to such a thing.

But why else would he have shot Bullard in the back?

Somehow, like a malicious parasite, doubt had invaded him, and he had killed Bullard outright rather than facing him man-to-man, the way he'd always faced the many, many others he'd killed.

His intention had been to unlock this younger Bullard, lead him out into the courtyard of the garrison, and put these troubling thoughts to rest by gunning him down in a fair contest.

That would wash away all thoughts of any vulnerability to doubt.

But now things had taken an unexpected turn. Something in Rose shifted as he told the sergeant to saddle the garrison's best horse.

The sergeant offered to ride out and fetch Ruelas for him, as did the coach driver when, with a horrified face, the man saw Rose mount the freshly saddled gelding, but Rose refused both offers.

Following the sergeant's directions, he rode off across the rough terrain, hating every jostle and bump of the loping horse.

By the time he discovered the lieutenant and his subordi-nates—one dead, the other chained ridiculously to his officer like an actor in a third-rate play—Rose had built up a touch of emotion he almost never allowed himself: anger.

"*Señor* Rose," Ruelas said, falling to his knees in a disgusting display of pitiful supplication. "*Señor*, I can explain!"

"Where is Bullard?"

"He surprised us, *Señor*, and shot at us from behind... like a coward."

Rose smiled. "Where is Bullard?"

"He stole my horse, *Señor*. Well, his horse, which I had commandeered. You see, we captured him, but—"

Rose shot him between the eyes, holstered the beautiful, custom-made, double-action Colt he had retrieved from the body of Frank Bullard, and smiled at the lieutenant's subor-dinate. "Where is Bullard?"

CHAPTER 37

I sabela's father, Ramon, drove the wagon slowly out the long and dusty road that led through *Don* Garza's gardens and orchards. Thanks to extensive irrigation, expert planning, and meticulous care this property was a beautiful oasis here in the Chihuahuan desert.

Three times, Ramon had passed crews of men tending the plants and trees and even raking the white pebbles that crunched beneath the hooves of the mules and the tires of the large wagon.

Coming around a corner, they saw a man on horseback blocking the road. This man was no gardener. Instead of a rake, he carried a rifle.

Ramon stopped the wagon.

"Where are you men going?" the man said, riding over.

"Good afternoon, *Señor,*" Ramon said with a smile. "We have come from Laguna Azul."

The man studied him for a moment. "I've seen you before."

"Yes, *Señor.* I have been here many times."

The man squinted at Coronado, who had exchanged his

178

Norteamericano clothing for simple peasant garb. "This one I do not remember."

"This is my nephew. It is his first time helping me."

"You don't look like a farmer," the man told Coronado.

"Looks can be deceiving, *amigo*," Coronado said. "Besides, I spend more time fishing than farming."

"May we pass, *Señor*?" Ramon asked. "We have goods for the *Don* to consider."

"If I did not know you, I would not let you pass," the man said, "but do not be surprised if the men at the gate turn you away. We are on high alert."

"What is wrong, *Señor*?"

The man shrugged. "I do not know, but we are to be watching out for a certain man, a tall *gringo* with green eyes. Have you seen such a man?"

They shook their heads. "Not ever in my life," Ramon said.

"Likewise," Coronado said, "but then again, I am just a farmer who likes to fish."

The guard laughed and waved them past. "Good luck, old man. Good luck, fisherman."

They thanked the guard and rode on in silence. There was nothing to say. They had already done everything possible to prepare for this moment. The previous night, Ramon and others—including Evelina, who had spent days within the walls and even the mansion itself—had drawn maps and explained everything they knew to Justice and Coronado.

When *Don* Garza's *hacienda* came into view, they could see many guards walking the parapet that ran along the inside of the ten-foot wall surrounding the compound. In each of the four corners, a tower rose twenty-five feet into the air. Two of these, including one in front, housed a Gatling gun.

Two men with rifles stood before the gate of heavy timbers.

One of the men stepped forward and scowled. "What do you peasants want?"

"We have driven all the way from Laguna Azul, *Señor*. We bring goods for the *Don* to consider."

"I've seen this man before," the other guard said, pointing at Ramon.

"Yes, *Señor*, I have been here many times. The *Don* appreciates things made by the people of my village, and today, we are in need of money."

The scowling man shook his head. "You will earn no money today. The *Don* is too busy to look at your rugs and *sarapes*. Come back in a week or two."

Ramon frowned. "If you insist, *Señor*. But you should know we do not carry our usual goods. Today, we have something very special."

"What do you have?" the friendlier guard asked.

"Pottery," Ramon said.

The scowling guard snorted. "Get out of here, old man. The *Don* doesn't need more plates."

"This is ancient pottery," Ramon said. "Very rare, very beautiful. Made by the old ones hundreds of years ago. My nephew found it in a cave."

Coronado nodded.

The friendlier guard stepped forward. "Let me see this pottery. My father has bought and sold such things in Janos."

He walked to the back of the wagon, pulled back the tarp, and poked around, obviously making sure they were carrying only pottery and no green-eyed *gringos*. Then he started examining the run-of-the-mill pottery that Justice had told them to cover in mud.

"This pottery is not special," the guard scoffed. "It is

merely dirty. Get out of here with your foolish tricks before you get yourself in trouble, old man."

"Some is new, some is old," Ramon said, fetching and unwrapping the bundle that had been riding at his feet. "See?"

He held out the ancient bowl Coronado had brought home from the Mogollon cave.

The guard studied it, a smile coming onto his face. To the scowling man, he said, "This is real. A perfect specimen."

"Yes," Ramon said, taking the bowl from him and rewrapping it with great reverence. "Now, may we please display our wares for the *Don*? As I have said, our village is in need of money."

"No," the first guard said. "Not today, old man. Come back in a week or two and perhaps then the *Don* will consider your pottery."

"We are sorry to trouble you, *Señor*," Ramon said. "We just know the *Don* appreciates fine things and with something so rare, we did not want him to be angry at us for not showing him first. But if you will not let us through, well, at least we tried. We will sell the pottery to someone else."

"Hold on," the guard who had examined the bowl said. He turned to his partner. "The old man speaks the truth. It is very old and very fine, very rare. A perfect artifact. Will the *Don* not be angry with us if we do not give him the opportunity?"

Grumbling, the first guard hollered to someone on the other side of the wall. "Open the gate!"

"*Muchas gracias, Señores*," Ramon said.

The high wooden doors swung wide, and Ramon drove into the cobblestone courtyard.

A hundred yards away at the center of the compound stood the magnificent mansion of *Don* Garza.

When Ramon thought of the man, he burned with rage,

wanting to gut him for what he had done to Isabela. He slowed two-thirds of the way to the *hacienda*, where he normally sold his goods.

"No," Coronado said. "Take us that way, closer to that tower."

"The guards will not like it."

"We will like it less if you park here and they kill us with the Gatling gun. Drive that way, *Tío*. Act natural." Saying this, Coronado reached beneath his seat and uncovered the things hiding there.

Noticing, Ramon removed the matches from his pocket.

"Hey, you!" the guard from inside the gate said, marching angrily toward them. "Listen to me, old man. Where are you going? Over there, where you normally go."

Ramon ignored the guard. He saw the men on the walls turning toward him, watching. His heart pounded. He knew this might be the last moment of his life. But he did not hesitate. If he died, at least he would die avenging the honor of his daughter, whom he loved more than anything in this cruel world.

They had drawn to within thirty-five yards of the tower. The Gatling gun was pointed away from them, of course, but the four men surrounding it stared down now, rifles in hand.

"Hey! Old man!" the gate guard hollered, running toward them now. "Are you deaf?"

"Five more yards, *Tío*," Coronado said. "Then stop the wagon and light the match."

Ramon rolled forward, pretending not to hear the shouting sentry, stopped twenty yards from the tower, and struck the match.

Coronado lifted the fuse to the match. Once it sparked to life, both men leapt into action.

Ramon drew the Winchester from beneath his seat and

opened fire on the shouting gate guard as Coronado jumped to his feet, drew the bow, and loosed the arrow.

Like all the men of his village, Coronado had grown up with a bow in his hands. Unlike those other men, he was also combat hardened and had spent hours the night before practicing for this moment.

Despite the stick of dynamite tied to its shaft, the arrow was true. It flew into the tower, among the men, who shouted briefly before the tower exploded, pitching their bodies into the air like so much shrapnel.

All around the courtyard, riflemen fired down from the walls.

Ramon fired back, retreating to the other side of the wagon, where Coronado had swapped out his bow for a rifle and where the dreaded green-eyed *gringo* had at last detached himself from the leather harnesses beneath the wagon, where he had been concealed with his weapons.

Bullets smashed into the wagon.

Ramon returned fire, knocking a man from the wall.

Ramon's body jerked and shuddered as if he'd been struck by lightning. Looking down, he saw the mess that was his right arm and realizing he could no longer fire the rifle, drew the pistol and began to fire left-handed as Justice sprinted back across the courtyard, zigging and zagging to avoid the gunfire.

CHAPTER 38

D on Antonio Garza had just made his selection when an explosion rocked the outer courtyard.

He had been pacing back and forth across the imported tiles of the mansion's inner courtyard, studying the line of young women like a general inspecting his ranks. Only, instead of standing up straight in starched uniforms, these girls trembled in their sheer gowns, too frightened to meet his eyes.

Their delicious fear invigorated him.

He would take one of these girls into the chamber of *lamentación*, transform her, and lift his spirits. In fact, he believed he would take another of the girls, perhaps even two, and force them to watch. He often did this. Spectators invariably worked even harder to please him after witnessing his work in the chamber.

"You," he said, just before the explosion, pointing to a girl whose name he couldn't remember. On one shapely leg a faint birthmark that had never bothered him now stood out, marking her as imperfect. "Come with me, my child."

He had just swept his eyes across the other girls, planning

to choose the spectators, when something exploded, and gunfire erupted outside his mansion.

Garza was no fool. Instantly, he knew what was happening.

Bullard was here.

Against all odds, the silent justice had come for him.

It didn't seem possible. The man was in custody. Rose had gone to deal with him.

How had Bullard escaped? How had he even figured out who and where Garza was?

Garza should have stayed in his beach house in Oaxaca. The girls were just as beautiful there, after all.

But some part of him—some very foolish part—had believed that this *hacienda*, being so remote and heavily guarded, would be plenty secure.

Now, Bullard was here.

And where was Rose?

The assassin had left for the garrison of the *Guardia Rural* this morning. Garza was expecting Rose to return any moment now with Bullard as his prisoner. In fact, he had even wondered if he would have time to finish playing with the girl before introducing Bullard to his chamber.

But now Bullard was here, and Rose wasn't, so *Don* Garza had to think quickly. He pulled his pocket pistol and gestured across the courtyard toward the archway that all the women knew and feared. "Everyone into the chamber."

The terrified girls complied, moving in front of him out of the courtyard and through the door into the mansion and down into the chamber.

They wept as they went, frightened by the explosion and gunfire but also no doubt terrified by their destination, because they had all either witnessed his work in the chamber or heard the tales of what he did there.

Bullard had unfortunately ruined Garza's plans, but the

girls were still of value to him. If the man somehow fought his way through Garza's guards—a highly unlikely possibility —and managed to find them down below, Garza would use the girls as hostages.

From what he understood, these silent justices, despite the horrific swaths of destruction they left in their wakes, nonetheless abided by codes of ethics. He would use Bullard's weakness against him, threatening the girls' lives if Bullard didn't let him go.

"Get over there by the back wall, where the chains hang down," he said impatiently, closing the door and throwing the bolt. Even with the bolt in place, however, he did not holster his pistol. Over one shoulder, he said, "Chain each other up. And stop crying, or I will give you something to cry about!"

CHAPTER 39

While Coronado and Ramon blasted away, providing cover, Justice charged the gate with a bundle of sparking dynamite.

Meanwhile, beyond the wall, the villagers who had ridden across the gardens and orchards opened fire, occupying the guards atop the parapets.

Justice hurled the dynamite, whirled around, and sprinted for the wagon.

Behind him, the dynamite exploded, shaking the ground and blasting the gate wide open.

Struck by the force of the blast and peppered with debris, Justice stumbled—and not a second too soon. As he fell forward, his hat leapt from his head, struck by a bullet that otherwise would have surely killed him.

He scrambled forward. Another round panged off the cobblestones just to one side, and then he was zigging and zagging again, weaving erratically as bullets cut the air around him.

Infiltrating the compound, destroying the Gatling gun, and blowing the gate had been necessary. Otherwise, the villagers wouldn't have stood a chance. Now, Justice and his friends needed to get out of this deathtrap of a courtyard and into the *hacienda*.

A passing bullet tugged at his shirt. Another creased him, igniting a line of fire across his buttocks.

"Come on!" he shouted to Coronado and Ramon, but coming around the wagon, he saw that both men were down… Ramon, sadly, for good.

Coronado tried to stand and fell again.

Even occupied as they were with the charging villagers, the men on the wall would finish Coronado easily unless Justice did something. So he sprinted behind the wagon and helped his friend to his feet.

Coronado was wounded in the side and the leg. "It's no good, Justice. Go ahead. I can't walk."

"You're *loco* if you think I'm leaving you here, *amigo*." Justice scooped the injured man over his shoulder and ran for the mansion.

Hurting bad, Coronado cursed with every bounce.

Behind them, the first of the villagers came smashing through the shattered gate and exchanged fire with the remaining guards.

Justice carried Coronado up the front steps and paused on the top landing to quickly adjust his hold and draw a Colt. When he went through the doors and into the stylish breezeway parlor, however, no one was waiting for him.

Now came the hard part: finding D.G.

Meanwhile, where was Rose?

Whatever the case, Justice had to help his friend first. He barged into a study with floor-to-ceiling shelves packed with leatherbound tomes and carried his groaning friend to a chair behind a large desk.

He holstered his Colt and lowered Coronado into the chair as gently as he could. Then he unbuckled his friend's belt and used it, along with Coronado's sheathed Bowie, to create a tourniquet above the leg wound.

Coronado cursed again as Justice tightened the tourniquet.

"I'm hit pretty hard, *amigo*," Coronado said. He looked very pale.

"Yeah. How's your side?" Justice asked, reaching into his pocket and pulling out one of the clean rags he'd packed in case something like this happened.

"Not good," Coronado said, accepting the rag and pressing it to the wound just below his ribcage.

"Keep pressure on that," Justice said, "and don't fall asleep or you'll never wake up."

Coronado chuckled through the pain. "You think I could sleep hurting like this?"

"Loosen that tourniquet from time to time," Justice told him, laying Coronado's six-shooter on the desk for him.

"I will, *amigo*. Go get Garza. And watch out for Rose."

Justice nodded and started for the door. He left his Colts holstered, unslung the 8 gauge, and headed back out into the hall.

CHAPTER 40

Her name was Anna Mendoza, and she had been born seventeen years earlier in a village a few hundred miles southwest of this terrible place, the youngest daughter of Ricardo and Paulina Mendoza. They lived a short walk from the Pacific Ocean, where her father fished for a living. Her parents were humble, much like their home, though her father earned enough money that they never went without, and Anna had eaten well enough to spring up, tall and shapely despite her youth.

Several local boys liked her and brought her little presents even though her father chased them all off, insisting that no village boy would ever be good enough for his daughter. Her father believed it was Anna's destiny to marry a great man and become wealthy, perhaps even famous.

Meanwhile, Anna just wanted to fish.

Her mother scolded her, worrying that Anna would tarnish her reputation. She should be a lady now. After all, what if some wealthy man passed through the village and spotted her?

Well, as it turned out, some wealthy man had indeed

spotted her. Or rather, his hired thugs had spotted and kidnapped her and brought her to this nightmare *hacienda* where she lived as the chattel of that wealthy man, the demon himself, *Don* Antonio Garza.

Nothing had seemed quite real since coming here. But it was real, as Anna reminded herself over and over every day, not wanting to lose touch the way the other girls had.

Of all of Garza's girls, Anna was the newest arrival. This made a difference. She was still the same person she had been in the village. She still remembered her old life. She had not slipped into denial and only feigned obeisance.

The other girls, however, were broken.

She stared at them in disbelief. Why were they obeying him?

Garza told them to chain each other up, and that's just what they were doing, even though they understood what he did to girls down here.

She shuddered—partly at the thought of his activities and partly to see these girls complying and assisting him, literally locking each other and themselves into shackles.

It was madness.

They were broken little fools.

But not Anna.

Garza wasn't even looking at them now perhaps because he was so frightened by what was happening outside or perhaps because he had come to expect total obedience from his captives and servants alike. He was staring at the bolted door, pointing the pistol at its heavy oak planks as if the attackers might come busting through any second.

She hoped they did. She hoped they burst through the door and killed him.

Was it her father? Had her father rallied the fishermen of her village and somehow managed to find her here?

She hoped so. But no matter who it was, she could not rely on them to save her now.

Seized by a powerful impulse, Anna swept a wooden bat from the table of unspeakable instruments, rushed forward, and struck *Don* Garza in the back of the head.

He wobbled, stunned but angry, and fired the pistol into the wall.

Deafened by the blast, Anna screamed and swung the bat again and again, pummeling the face of her would-be torturer as he fired the pistol once more.

CHAPTER 41

Wh... hen four men with drawn pistols came shouting around the corner, Justice gave them both barrels. At this range, the buckshot filled the corridor. Packed tightly together, Garza's guards didn't stand a chance.

Justice was about to reload when he heard more shouting and the footsteps of what sounded like several men running his way from both directions. Just how many guards did Garza have?

Slinging the 8 gauge over his shoulder, Justice stepped into a storage room and drew both Colts.

A second later, two men carrying rifles appeared down the hall to the right twenty yards away. Justice stepped into the hall, putting both pistols on the men. "Put down the rifles," he told them in Spanish.

The men shouldered their weapons, swinging the barrels toward him.

He pulled both triggers, striking the men center mass and putting them down.

At that moment, shouting filled the hall to his left, where

three men jerked to a stop before the quartet he'd killed with the scattergun.

One of them spotted him, shouted, and lifted a pistol.

Justice shot him first and told the others to surrender.

But apparently, Don Garza only employed bullheaded men with outsized notions of themselves because these guards also ignored his warning and opened fire.

Their shots went wide.

Justice's didn't.

When both men were down, he paused to reload and holster his Colts, then broke open the 8 gauge, reloaded, snapped the barrels shut, and started down the hall.

In the outer courtyard, the shooting had slowed. He knew that some of the villagers, armed with the rifles he had captured from the *rurales*, had breached the wall. Others were to remain outside the walls, sticking to the front of the compound, keeping the back tower Gatling gun out of the fight.

Pausing at a window, he peered outside and saw a wonderful sight: the villagers charging forward unmolested, ready to enter the *hacienda*. Among them, he saw Coronado's father, who had ridden with Geronimo against the Spanish. Now, the man's brother, Ramon, lay dead in the courtyard, and his son lay badly wounded in Garza's study.

Justice hoped Coronado's father found his son before it was too late. He also hoped the younger Coronado didn't shoot his father and friends when they came through the door.

Whatever the case, he had to leave them to it and go find Garza and Rose.

He looked through the window on the other side of the hall. The inner courtyard remained empty.

He walked down the hall, stepping over the many bodies, and risked a quick glimpse into the adjoining corridor.

Seeing no one, he entered the hall and started down it, shotgun at the ready.

He checked each room, hunting for his quarry.

In the kitchen, a woman saw him and cowered, raising her hands as if they might shield her if he pulled the triggers. "*No me mates!*" she begged.

Justice swung the barrels away from the frightened woman. "I won't kill you. Where's Garza?"

"He is below."

"Where?"

"The room beneath the ground," she said with a shudder. "It is a bad place, *Señor*. He took the women there. I saw him out the window."

"Show me."

"Will you kill him, *Señor*?"

Justice nodded.

"Then I will show you," she said, and led him back out into the hall.

CHAPTER 42

Don Antonio Garza awoke to the worst headache of his life. At first, he was confused. Then he saw the girls and the chamber around them, and in a moment of terrifying clarity he understood everything.

One of these traitorous wenches—the new girl; what was her name?—had struck him from behind. He remembered the ensuing struggle, remembered trying to shoot her, remembered the bat smashing down in his face, filling his head with sparks… and then, nothing.

Nothing, that is, until now. And oh, seeing things clearly, how he wished he could return to that sweet nothingness.

He was lying on his back, strapped in place.

The new girl, the one who had hit him, leaned into view, pointing the pistol at his face.

He tried to flinch away but could barely move within the restraints. Only then did he realize where he was lying. They had secured him to the very same table he used to transform those he brought to the chamber of *lamentación*.

"No," he said, hating the panic in his voice. He was the *Don*, after all, and these were merely peasant girls. He should speak with authority, and they should do his bidding. That was the way of the world. Until this horrible woman had betrayed him. "What are you doing? I demand you release me!"

The girl with the pistol pressed its muzzle against his forehead. The other girls leaned close, leering down at him with gleaming eyes. They looked nothing like themselves, nothing like the timid girls who cavorted for him. They looked like demons.

"Wait!" he begged. "Stop! Don't shoot me!"

Pulling the pistol away, the girl said, "Don't worry, *Don* Garza. We will not shoot you."

He sighed. "Good. That is good."

"After all," the girl continued, "you did not shoot Rosa."

Rosa? He thought. *Who was Rosa? One of these girls?*

"You didn't shoot Juana," another girl said.

His confusion deepened. *Who was Juana?*

A girl with wide, terrifying eyes stepped forward. It was the girl with the birthmark. Seeing the terrible look on her face, he was glad he had not explained his plans for her. "You did not shoot my sister, Gabriela."

Her sister? Oh yes... her sister. This was one of those two girls his men had taken together this fall. Panic erupted in him. He had killed her sister. Killed her here upon this very table.

"Release me," he blurted, overcome by fear. "I will do anything. I will give you anything."

"You will give us everything," the girl he'd been meaning to kill said, holding up a silver scalpel, "just as you took everything from my sister."

Even before the cold steel touched *Don* Garza's flesh, his screams filled the chamber of *lamentación*.

197

"What are your names?" Justice asked the poor women, his heart breaking for them as they emerged from the chamber, finally understanding that their nightmare was over.

Speaking of nightmares, the scene he had beheld in the subterranean chamber would certainly haunt him for years to come. But justice had been served. There was no doubt about that.

Yes, the girls had done unspeakable things to *Don* Antonio Garza, killing him in the process; but Justice understood that Garza had not only deserved this end but had also, through his own unfathomable cruelty, made the girls capable of doing what they had done.

Garza had created monsters. And then the monsters had destroyed their creator.

Perhaps now, with Garza dead, these girls could return to their homes, put this all behind them, and rediscover their humanity.

"My name is Anna," the one with the pistol said, and she told him she was from a small fishing village.

"We will get you back to your home," Justice assured her. "We will get all of you back to your homes."

The battle was over. There were no more gunshots.

Coming back into the courtyard, Justice rendezvoused with Coronado's father and a few smiling villagers. They had two prisoners.

Better yet, they brought news that Coronado remained alive and conscious. His father believed his son would survive. One of the men they had captured upon entering the *hacienda* was a doctor, and he was attending to the younger Coronado now.

"What do we do with these prisoners?" the elder Coronado asked.

"That man came to my village and kidnapped me," Anna said, pointing to one of the bound men.

"Yes," another girl said. "He came to my village, too."

The other girls chimed in, agreeing about this man, who started pleading for his life. One girl pointed out that he had also killed her brother when taking her.

To Coronado's father, Justice said, "We need a rope and a tree. Can you handle this matter, *Señor* Coronado?"

"Gladly, *Señor*. What about this other man? Should I fetch a second rope?"

Justice regarded the other man. He was young, wounded, and trembling. To the women, Justice said, "Do you recognize this man?"

They recognized him but only as a guard. None of them had seen him do anything wrong.

"No second rope," Justice said. "Take this man away and keep an eye on him, but I expect to release him once we are finished here. If he was merely a hired guard, no further justice is warranted."

"Thank you, *Señor*," the pardoned man said. "Thank you for sparing my life."

"I have a question for you," Justice told the guard. Garza was dead, the girls were freed, and the battle was over, but his work was not finished yet. "Where is *el último hombre*? Where is Rose?"

"I'm here," a deep voice said, as a smiling, well-dressed man entered the courtyard at gunpoint. "You must be Jake Bullard."

Justice nodded, taking in Rose as the killing frost settled over him afresh. Here before him, wrists bound, helpless as a lamb before slaughter, was the man who had killed his father.

"We stopped his coach as they were coming down the road," one of his captors said.

"You didn't fight them?" Justice said.

Rose shook his head. "There were too many of them. They had me on both sides. With rifles, no less. At that range, pulling my six-shooters would have been suicide." He smiled again. "Besides, I assumed they would lead me to you, and I was correct."

"And why would that be a good thing?" Justice asked.

"Because I'm going to kill you, of course."

"Fool!" one of the villagers said, lifting his rifle. "Shall I kill him, *Señor* Justice?"

Rose awaited Justice's answer with a knowing smile.

"No," Justice said. "Him and me have unfinished business."

"Excellent," Rose said. "I've been looking forward to this. And when I defeat you, will I be set free?"

Justice shook his head and spoke to the riflemen. "I don't plan on him beating me, but if he does, shoot him. The man needs to die for his crimes. Now, spread out and have your rifles ready. They say he's quick."

The elder Coronado touched Justice's arm. "You're going to fight him, *Señor*? Why take the chance?"

It was a good question, a question that had been whispering in various forms across Justice's thoughts for a long time. What was justice? Was he truly its embodiment or was he just a man doing his best with its dispensation? Would it be just to gun down a man such as Rose, the killer for hire who'd murdered Justice's father, without giving him a chance? Or would that make Justice a murderer, too?

Justice didn't know the answers to these questions, but sometimes you know what you have to do without needing to know why.

"He killed my Pa. Now I'm gonna kill him. Go ahead, set him loose, and give his guns back. You folks best back away. Him and me are gonna settle our differences right here, right now."

CHAPTER 44

The two men faced each other across the courtyard, a mere 15 yards apart. Men of their skill would not miss at this range. Everything would come down to speed.

Coronado's father would give the command to draw.

But first, they had words.

"I've been looking forward to this moment," Rose said.

"You've been looking forward to dying?"

"Dying is nothing to me, Bullard. Killing is everything. I enjoyed killing your father, but I'm going to enjoy killing you even more." His pencil mustache curled with his bright smile. "And I must say that I have come to appreciate your father's pistols. The trigger pull is the best I've ever seen on a double action. They were clearly custom made at the Colt factory. Tell me, do all silent justices carry these?"

Justice stared back at his opponent. By talking about Justice's father, Rose was trying to rattle him. It wouldn't work. Yes, he wanted very badly to kill Rose, but facing such a proficient killer, he couldn't afford anger or tension. So he dismissed all emotion and said, "This isn't about the silent justices. This is personal. You ready, Rose?"

"Yes, I am ready," Rose said with a chuckle, "but there is one more thing you should know before I kill you."

"What's that?"

"I sent two men to your home."

Despite the steel in Justice's soul, this one rattled him. "What are you talking about?"

"I sent McSweeney and Banderas to your ranch. By now, they've killed your children and had their way with your wife. They've taken her to Socorro. And if they don't hear from me by tonight, they'll kill her, too."

"You lie."

Rose shook his head. "Dos Pesos, New Mexico, right? I never lie, Mr. Bullard."

"Well, I do," Justice said. "And after I kill you, I'll send these men a telegram... with your name on it, of course. *Señor* Coronado, if I am killed, will you see the telegram is sent to McSweeney and Banderas in Socorro? Tell them to come back here to the *hacienda*. Lie in wait, save my wife, and kill these men."

Coronado nodded. "It shall be done, *Señor*. The Apaches taught me how to make an enemy suffer. These men will scream before they die."

Rose chuckled. "Well played, Mr. Bullard. What do you say we get down to it? After shooting your father in the back, I've been wanting to kill a Bullard face-to-face. Funny, as he was dying, your father didn't say a word about you. Just kept asking for Matt."

These psychological attacks missed their target. Justice was ready and wouldn't let Rose confuse things. He settled his right hand onto his Colt and nodded to Coronado.

Coronado looked back and forth between the combatants and lifted a hand above his head. "Draw!" he shouted, slicing the air with his hand.

Justice and Rose drew at the same instant.

Rose fired, jerked with impact, threw himself to the right, and fired again.

Justice fired, twisted his body sideways, felt Rose's bullet strike his chest, and fired again.

Rose's second shot raced across the courtyard and smashed a vase sitting atop a pedestal.

Justice's second shot nailed the infamous gunfighter in the pencil mustache and rid the world of Rose forever.

The men around the courtyard cheered.

The young woman named Anna rushed forward. "Are you all right, *Señor*?"

Justice raised a hand to his burning chest. He believed Rose had struck him with a glancing blow. But then again, he'd been hurt before without knowing how serious it was until the moment had ended and he'd had time to check himself.

His shirt was warm and wet with blood, and some part of his chest had come loose. He could feel it sliding down his shirt, which he began to unbutton, knowing there was a chance he'd sprung a leak that would end him.

At least Garza was dead, the women were safe, and he had avenged his father by killing Rose. Even if he died now, he had set things right, and these folks would do what they could to save Nora in case Rose's story really was true, which he kindly doubted. If his children were dead and his wife was in peril, Justice would feel it right in his heart.

Spreading his shirt, he looked down at his chest. There was plenty of blood, but he laughed at the star-shaped wound where Rose's bullet had knocked the badge from his flesh.

"Yeah, I'm okay," he told the girl, fishing the bloody badge from within his shirt.

"I am so glad, *Señor* Justice," Anna said, then furrowed her brow with confusion. "Or is it *Señor* Bullard?"

Smiling down at the half-melted badge that had been part of him since he'd been reborn by the river, he said, "I reckon it's time for me to figure that out."

CHAPTER 45

Fredericksburg, Texas; spring, 1884

Hill country glowed, alive with bluebonnets in full bloom. The morning was bright and sunny and warm—a perfect day for a wedding.

Though any day is perfect for a wedding, Justice thought, watching Nora walk from room to room in the Bullard ranch house, taking everything in with a beautiful smile, *if you're lucky enough to marry a woman you love more than life itself.*

Spending the winter with Nora and the children had been wonderful, and now Nora was more beautiful than ever because she was beginning to show with the child they had indeed conceived immediately after marriage.

Justice liked to imagine conception had occurred on their wedding night rather than the strange and violent honeymoon they had taken to New York City, a place he didn't want associated with his child in any way; but in the end, he supposed it didn't matter when the child had begun to exist, just as it did not matter whether they had a son or daughter. Whatever the case, he would love this child as much as he loved Eli and Katie… in other words, with every fiber of his mind, body, and soul.

The winter had been good for other reasons, too.

His wounds had healed as had the wounds of many others. Mostly, anyhow.

Some, like Ramon, were gone forever, and others would spend the rest of their lives trying to overcome the traumatic things they had endured; but Coronado was mostly healed, and Matt was on his feet again and had surprised doctors by regaining use of his badly wounded arm.

The ranch in Dos Pesos thrived as Justice and Nora learned to ranch on a larger scale. They had hired more hands, including a one-armed ex-miner who worked for a dollar a month… if you could call it working.

Clem actually knew a thing or two about horses and did make himself useful from time to time, but mostly he just hung around the bunkhouse cracking jokes and asking when the next meal was going to be, insisting that Katie's cooking had surpassed even the fine cuisine of A. Lapierce, the fancy chef the Clarendon Hotel in Leadville, had poached from Delmonico's in New York.

Justice wouldn't disagree. Katie had grown to be quite the cook, quite the daughter, and quite the sister. She was the happiest girl he'd ever seen, living in a loving home with her new family and her very own bedroom, surrounded by books.

The winter had also been a time for romance, and not just between Justice and Nora.

Shortly after Christmas, Justice had received a letter from Kansas. It read,

Dear Jake,

Well, I did it. I bought the farm I grew up on, and I'm in the

process of fixing it all up. I have big hopes for this little place, so I'm working hard, but I couldn't be happier, especially because my husband, Mr. Charles Baxter, treats me so well and works so hard.

Charles and I met at church through my family, with whom I have completely reconciled. I cannot believe how good things are, Jake. Thank you so much for all your help and, of course, for believing in me. If you and your family ever visit Kansas, Charles and I would love to have you all for dinner.

Fondly,

Lilly

P.S. I KNOW YOU ARE GRINNING AND SAYING, "I TOLD YOU SO." SEE the attached. Our wager is complete. Lilly Baxter pays her debts!

AND THERE, FASTENED BY A DAB OF RED WAX TO THE LETTER, was the penny she had promised to pay should she be married as Justice had predicted.

He was very happy for her and very happy for Luke and Faith, whose wedding had brought his family to Fredericksburg today.

Justice had proudly accepted his cousin's request to stand beside him during the ceremony, and he knew Nora would be overjoyed to stand beside her little sister Faith.

"I love this place, Justice," Nora said, coming back into the room. "I really do. It's a joy to imagine you, your father, and Matt living here."

He nodded at that. "I'm glad I'm starting to remember more."

That was another of this winter's many blessings. He was finally beginning to remember his past. It was nice returning to Fredericksburg and remembering folks' names when they greeted him. It was even nicer to remember growing up with Matt, but best of all was remembering Pa.

"Oh," Nora said, drifting over to where the large Bible sat on a pedestal near the wall. She turned a bright smile on Justice, who managed not to wince as she ran her fingertips over the cover of the Bible. "I am positively overjoyed to find a Bible in the Bullard home!"

Then Nora opened the good book, gasped, and raised a hand to her chest. With her other hand, she plucked the tiny pistol from inside and turned to him smiling and shaking her head. "You Bullards and your weapons."

"Well, my love, you're a Bullard now, too, and if I'm not mistaken, your weapons have come in handy more than once already."

Nora laughed. "That is true." She replaced the small pistol and closed the cover. "But I insist on getting Matt another Bible while we're in town."

Justice couldn't think about what had almost happened at the ranch in Dos Pesos, and he thanked God every day that Nora and good old Rafer had taken care of Rose's rogues.

Garza's operation had burned to the ground. Searching the *hacienda*, Justice had found not only a massive amount of money, most of which went to Coronado's village and the girls Garza had victimized, but also heaps of valuable information, including names, locations, and ledgers.

He had passed this information to Matt, who shared it with Doc. American and Mexican authorities were informed, and soon after, raids started on both sides of the border. According to Matt, hundreds of girls had returned to their families.

Justice was incredibly happy to have played a part in freeing these poor girls, but his own relationship with the silent justices remained in limbo. He hadn't heard word one from Doc or the commander, though he expected to see the former at Luke's wedding later that day.

Nora was worried that Doc might use their reunion to apprehend Justice, but Justice assured her that Doc would never use a wedding to trap him. Doc would at least give Justice a warning and a head start before beginning the hunt.

How Justice hoped that never came to pass. He loved his life on the ranch with Nora and the kids. He had never dreamed he could be so happy.

And yet, truth be told, some nights when he awoke with the winter wind howling down off the mountain and making the house creak and groan, he would lie awake and stare up into the darkness, feeling curiously detached from the world.

Not detached from Nora or the children, of course. Never that. But he felt out of step with his purpose and, perhaps even his true identity.

That question had been much on his mind since his duel with Rose. The wound had healed, and he kept the badge with him always—had it in the pocket of his trousers at the moment, in fact—but he still didn't have the answer to who he really was.

Maybe he never would.

For now, it was enough to love his wife and children and to never stop feeling grateful for their health and happiness and every second he got to spend with them.

He drew Nora into his arms and kissed her long and deeply, cherishing every second.

Then the children, as children are wont to do, came barging in.

"Pa," Katie said, still holding a purring Tilly to her chest. "Eli and I have something to ask you."

"Can we bring the cat home, Pa?!" Eli blurted.

"Well, that all depends on your Uncle Matt. She's more his cat now than mine."

"Hogwash," Matt said, coming in from outside. "That there is a one-man cat. Take her with you. She's too lazy to catch mice anyway, and she talks so much, she about drives me crazy."

The children cheered and turned to their parents. "Is that okay, Pa?" Katie asked.

Justice nodded.

"Is it okay by you, Ma?" Eli asked.

Smiling, Nora said, "Sure, but you'd better watch out that Rafer doesn't gobble her up."

"Aw, Rafer wouldn't hurt a fly," Eli said, and they all burst out laughing. Then, realizing maybe he'd exaggerated things a bit, Eli said, "Well, not unless the fly had it coming."

"All right, Bullards," Matt said, "you ready to head to the wedding or what?"

CHAPTER 46

The wedding, like the bride, was beautiful.

Justice couldn't be happier for Luke and Faith. During the whole ceremony, he focused on their smiling faces, his heart brimming over with love.

Despite this fact, he was also aware of the compact man who entered the church and took a seat in the back just as the preacher started talking.

Now, with the wedding over, Justice congratulated the newlyweds and leaned close to kiss Nora on the cheek. Tasting the salt of happy tears she'd shed for her baby sister, he whispered, "If you'll excuse me for a second, I gotta go talk to Doc."

Nora embraced him. "I love you, Justice. And no matter what he says, no matter what it means for us, the kids and I are with you till the end of time."

"Well, in that case, all the pressure is off, darlin. Because if I'm with you and the kids, I'm the happiest man in the world."

Justice followed Doc out of the church. He had remembered more about the man over recent months. Doc was fair but absolutely strict, the embodiment not only of justice but also integrity, and unequivocally deadly.

Outside, Doc turned and smiled. He'd known Justice was behind him, of course. Doc was always aware of everything and everyone. "Jake," he said, and offered his hand.

Justice shook it. "Doc."

"Nice wedding."

Justice nodded. "They're good people."

"Speaking of good people, we're in the process of choosing another silent justice."

That did not bode well. Justice braced himself for the rest of it. "You're replacing me, then?"

"No, we're aiming to fill the vacancy left by your father... whom I understand you have avenged."

"Yes sir, I have."

Doc nodded, staring into the distance. "You made quite a stir down there in Mexico. Quite a stir. The president was angrier than a bull that kicked a beehive."

"I imagine so." Justice knew he'd caused an international incident. Some of it was in the papers—everything was fairly vague, of course, except for the Mexican president's anger with the United States—and some of it he had heard from Matt.

"But once the president started receiving reports on all you achieved down there," Doc said, "all the girls you saved, all the corruption you rooted out, well, he changed his tune. So did the Mexican president for that matter, though, of course, they would never put that in the papers. Trouble sells more copies than satisfaction, no matter which side of the border you're on."

"Well, I'm glad to hear it."

Doc nodded. "Yeah, I suppose you are."

For a moment, neither man spoke.

Then Doc reached into his suit coat, withdrew an envelope, and handed it to Justice. "Commander sent this to me. Talk it over with your wife and let me know what you're gonna do."

Their eyes met for a brief second, and Doc touched the brim of his hat. "Good seeing you, Jake. Nice family you got there."

As Doc walked off, Justice opened the envelope, knowing whatever waited inside would change his life forever.

The letter was addressed to Doc. It read:

THE PRESIDENT OF THE UNITED STATES IS QUITE IMPRESSED BY *Silent Justice Jake Bullard. He grants Bullard a full pardon on all counts; and I, as Commander of the Silent Justices, grant Bullard a marriage exemption, both conditions to be enacted immediately and irrevocably so long as Jake Bullard agrees to continue serving in his lifelong post as a silent justice.*

JUSTICE READ THE LETTER AGAIN, THEN READ IT ONCE MORE.

He looked across the courtyard to where Nora waited beside their children, the perfect picture of domestic bliss.

That very instant, Nora looked up at him and smiled in that wise way she had, and he walked over to her and handed her the letter.

She didn't open it. "I already know what it says."

"You do?"

"I reckon I do."

"How?"

"Woman's intuition. Let me guess… all is well as long as you go back to working for them?"

He nodded, once again impressed by his amazing wife.

"What do you aim to do?" Nora asked.

"Well, I've been real happy sticking around the ranch with

you and the kids these last few months, but—" He paused, the enormity of the decision rearing up before him.

"Do it, Justice," Nora said, holding him by the arms and smiling up at him. "Go back to work with them. Not because I don't want to live life on the run but because it's who you are. We have loved having you home with us, too, and we will cherish every second we spend with you when you aren't tracking down bad men, but you weren't just born to serve justice, my love. You were also *reborn* to serve it. And for as much as the children and I need you, the West needs you, too. Do it, Justice."

They embraced, Justice's heart feeling like it might burst he loved this woman and their children so much.

"I'll do it, then," he told her, knowing this was the right decision, knowing that this was who he was... not just a family man or a hunter of bad men but both things at the same time. "I'll be gone here and there, sometimes maybe even for weeks at a time, but mostly, I'll be home with you and the kids."

"Good," Nora said. "We will love having you home... and may God have mercy on those who earn your wrath."

———

hear about new releases, special sales, and giveaways, join my reader list.

Once more, thanks for reading. I hope our paths cross again.

Until then, don't approach a bull from the front, a horse from the rear, or a fool from any direction.

ABOUT THE AUTHOR

I was born six months before man landed on the moon and lucky enough to grow up in the country, where my family lived largely off the land.

When I wasn't fishing, exploring the woods, or weeding the garden, I devoured comic books like *Two-Gun Kid* and *The Rawhide Kid* before moving on to the exciting adventure stories of Jack London and Louis L'Amour.

Our black-and-white TV only got three channels, though you could lose one and pick up another if you went outside and messed with the antenna. On its grainy screen, we watched *Gunsmoke*, *Bonanza*, and movies starring John Wayne and Clint Eastwood.

Now a husband and father, I love traveling the West and reading history and fiction alike. My favorite authors are Louis L'Amour, Elmore Leonard, C.J. Petit, and R.O. Lane.

As a writer, I hope to entertain you with fun stories of the old West. My good guys are good, my bad guys are bad, and you'll always find a touch of romance to sweeten the grit.

If you'd like to keep in touch, join my newsletter HERE.

ALSO BY JOHN DEACON

Made in the USA
Coppell, TX
24 October 2023